# BEFORE

Jared's Story,
Forlorn Series
Prequel

## GINA DETWILER

Vinspire Publishing
www.vinspirepublishing.com

This book is dedicated to Dawn Carrington,
who made it happen.

# PART ONE

# Genesis

When human beings began to
increase in number on the earth
and daughters were born to them,
the sons of God saw that
the daughters of humans were beautiful,
and they married any of them they chose.
*Genesis 6:1-2*

# Chapter One

On September 2, 1859, a massive solar flare struck the earth's atmosphere, touching off the biggest geomagnetic storm in recorded history. Telegraph systems all over the world failed as telegraph poles burst into flame and operators were hospitalized with electric burns. Had this storm, known as the Carrington Event, occurred a hundred years later, it would have plunged much of the world into darkness.

Most people did not know about solar flares and didn't use the telegraph, but what they saw in the sky took their breath away. Brilliant auroras of red, green, and purple blazed as far south as the Caribbean, so bright that coal miners in Colorado got up in the middle of the night and started making breakfast. For a time, the entire world seemed enveloped in marvelous, colorful, undulating light, a celestial cloud of impossible delicacy. A gold miner in Australia described the aurora as a thing of "unspeakable beauty…a sight never to be forgotten." And then, in a moment of prescience, he added, "The rationalist and pantheist saw nature in her most exquisite robes, recognizing, the divine immanence. The superstitious and the fanatical had dire forebodings, and thought it a foreshadowing of Armageddon and final dissolution."

I was born on September 2, 1859.

I often wondered what my mother thought as she labored in the home of her husband's parents in Saint-Genis-Pouilly, a tiny French hamlet a stone's throw from Switzerland. Did she fear the sort of creature she would birth? For like the auroras that lit the sky over her bed, I was an unforeseen phenomenon, a product of nature turned unnatural, a dreadful secret that must be kept hidden from the world.

My parents were circus performers, and the circus was the perfect place to hide. No one paid much attention to a small child amid half-naked bareback riders, lion tamers, acrobats and dancing clowns. No one noticed that I never seemed to grow, that I was still no more than a toddler at ten years old, although I could talk like a much older child. My parents were part of a small, itinerant circus that traveled the towns and villages of southern France. Provence, Avignon, Nîmes, Bourg en-Brêsse, many more long forgotten now.

A flamboyant gypsy named Maurice Bourgnon ran the circus—his wife, his six brothers, two mistresses and seventeen children made up the bulk of the performers. My parents were among the few hired talent. My father trained my mother to do tricks on the backs of white horses as they galloped around the ring. She wore a white sequined costume with feathery angel wings that flapped as she twirled and flipped. It was the most popular act in the show, until my father discovered a new act that was sweeping circuses all over France.

The trapeze.

My father believed that this was the future of the circus. He built a tall, wooden frame rigged with a swing and began training my mother to do aerial acrobatics. She was a natural and learned quickly, so he built a thirty-foot frame that fit inside the big tent. I will never forget the first time I saw my mother fly on the high trapeze—her effortless grace seemed to me a kind of magic.

Never satisfied, my father built a second trapeze so that he and my mother could swing in synchronization. Their tricks became more dangerous and thrilling, my mother leaping from her swing, twirling in the air and catching my father's arms. His immense physical strength made their death-defying act all the more awe-inspiring. But it was the image of them together that seared my memory: my father dressed in glittering black, playing the devil to my mother's luminous angel. They called themselves Lucas and Charmaine, the Divine Duo.

We traveled eight months a year from village to village, living in a cramped, rickety wagon that doubled as our transportation. Later on, the circus traveled by train, but in those early days the railroad system was not as extensive as it would later become. I loved the animals especially: the horses, the dogs, the monkeys, and even the old lion named Nero, so fat he could hardly walk without dragging his belly on the ground. Yet what a roar he could produce before a crowd!

Whenever I could, I helped the animal keepers by filling the water buckets. When no one was looking, I would stick my hand into Nero's cage to touch the matted fur of his mane. He'd swing his big head around to look at me, his eyes all droopy and bloodshot, and let out a half-hearted roar.

I was supposed to stay in the wagon during the performances, but I often snuck out to watch my parents perform. I longed to be a part of the show. *Someday*, my mother said. *Never*, said my father. It wasn't just because of my size, I knew. Smaller children than I performed in the circus. There was something about me that my father disdained, something that made him afraid.

"Why does he hate me?" I asked my mother once.

She hugged me, told me not to worry. "You will grow. You will be strong. It will just take you a little longer."

I decided to prove to him I could be a performer, that I was worthy of being his son. One early morning I went into the big tent, climbed up the rope to the top of the trapeze. My breath caught as I stared at the floor below—it was much farther down than I had expected. I wasn't afraid. I felt exhilarated. I grabbed hold of the bar and swung into the air. It was glorious, that feeling of flying, untethered to the earth. I swung and swung, pumping my little legs, going up so high I could touch the top of the circus tent with my feet.

I don't know how long I was swinging, for then I heard a cry from below. "Jean-Luc! Jean-Luc! What are you doing? Someone help!" Other voices soon joined the first. And then my father's voice.

"Jean-Luc! Take my hand!"

He had climbed up the rope and stretched out his arm, ready to grab me when I swung close to him. His face was a mask of fury and I knew what I was in for if he caught me. So I let go. I heard screams and gasps from below—there was no net. I felt the air under me buoying my descent. I spread my arms and did a flip before landing on my feet.

Dozens of people stared at me in shocked silence. What I'd done was impossible. Yet it had seemed the most natural thing in the world to me.

"Jean-Luc!" My mother rushed to me, gathered me in her arms. She was trembling. "Don't ever do that again."

"Why not?"

"You could have been killed!"

"I don't think so."

She gave me a look I'd never seen before, one of abject terror.

I tried to obey my mother, but I was hooked on the trapeze. I learned to be more secretive. I went to the ring while my parents slept and the gypsies were laughing and drinking in the ringmaster's wagon. I swung until my arms ached, trying to imitate my parents' most difficult tricks. The dark didn't bother me. I loved it—sailing through a void.

For many weeks I went undetected. But then one night Monsieur le Blanc, the lead clown in the circus, came out of the shadows after one of my more spectacular landings, clapping his hands in slow rhythm. In the ring, Monsieur le Blanc, or "Blanky" as he was known on stage, wore a loose white shirt with a red ruffled collar, and leggings speckled with large red flowers made of tulle. With his face smothered in white paint, he wore a white, cone-shaped hat with a tassel. He was an excellent mime and also performed funny acts with his little dog, Sniffy. Sniffy didn't like me, and growled whenever I came near, so I stayed away from them both.

"Look what I have found." The clown leered at me. Beside him, Sniffy growled low and bared his teeth. Without his makeup, Blanky's face was mottled and much older than I expected, his smile wide and virtually toothless. "Such a little boy doing such marvelous things."

I backed away, but he kept closing the gap between us.

"How talented you are. Why do your parents hide you? Why do they not let you perform?"

I didn't answer.

"I guess they don't think much of you, do they? Perhaps they would allow me to make you a part of my act. I'll make you a costume, just like mine. Petit Le Blanc. You'd be in disguise, no one would know who you are. You could do tricks, all sorts of tricks. I know you can. Leaping and balancing and flipping. I've been watching you for many nights. You will soon be the star of the show. What do you say?"

I still said nothing, just shook my head. The man's breath was rancid, his face so close to mine I could smell the greasepaint in the folds of his skin.

"You do not speak? Well then, perhaps I must tell your father about your escapades in the night."

I shook my head.

"I think I must. He should know what his *little* boy is up to." The way he emphasized *little* chilled me. "I think I could make a nice arrangement with him. I will keep silent, as a good clown does, if he allows you into my act. What do you think?"

I stared at the ground.

"No voice! My, my, my. You will make a very good clown. Let us see what your father has to say."

He hurried off, Sniffy at his heels.

That was the last time anyone saw Monsieur Le Blanc. He did not show up in the breakfast line the next morning. His clown friends laughed, thinking he had drunk too much the night before. But I knew better.

The ring master was enraged at the clown's disappearance. How dare his best clown desert the circus in the middle of the night, with no word to anyone? There were those who suspected something unfortunate had happened to Monsieur Le Blanc, but no one went looking for him. No police report was filed. The circus simply moved on.

My father never spoke of the clown. But from that night on, he made me sleep in an empty animal cage with a padlock on the door.

# Chapter Two

When I was eighteen (though I looked to be about three), my parents joined the Cirque d'Hiver, the pinnacle of the circus world in the center of Paris—a massive oval amphitheater modeled after the Colosseum in Rome, that operated in the winter when all other circuses were shut down.

I was awestruck by this magnificent building, grander than any I had dared to imagine. The trapeze itself was twice as tall as our old one, with steel poles attached to the ceiling, and a ladder and platform in addition to the two swings. My parents were able to expand their act and add even more tricks. They were still quite fit and agile despite being in their late thirties—their performances soon became the highlight of the show.

I could no longer sneak swings on the trapeze, for the ring was never empty. Every day but Sunday boasted three performances, with rehearsals in between. Some performers even practiced in the middle of the night and slept between shows during the day. But since my father was so preoccupied with the act, I was free to roam where I wanted and find other companions fill my days.

The circus barker, Leroy, was my favorite. He was a former clown with a crinkly, animated face who went up and down the street coaxing people to come to the show. I would accompany him, holding a sign that listed the performance times while he danced around, juggled walnuts, pulled fake flowers from the pockets of passersby and generally made a fool of himself. Even I was something of an attraction—women would stop to pat my head and exclaim, "Such a beautiful child!" Sometimes they gave me pennies, which I handed over to Leroy. He rewarded me with little pieces of sticky candy that had been in his pockets for months.

Other days, I played hide and seek with the "circus brats" in the cavernous tunnels and hallways of the amphitheater. During the shows, I would crawl up into the access shafts meant for lighting the gas chandeliers and watch through the peepholes in the ceiling. I was small enough and agile enough to do this so quickly not even the gas engineer saw me. From there I had a spectacular view of the arena as well as the audience. I spied artists like George Seurat and Henri de Toulouse-Lautrec—men who would later become famous—sketch away with their charcoal and pastels. Many of those paintings now hang in museums—priceless works of art—and I saw them being born.

We lived in a townhouse a few blocks from the circus, which was much roomier than the old wagon. I had my own room—my father no longer locked me in the animal cages at night. He still did his best to pretend I didn't exist, but that was fine with me. I was good at hiding, staying out of his way.

My mother took me to Parisian doctors, eager to find a cure for my condition, or at least an explanation. When she told them my actual age, they refused to believe it. Yet they prescribed all manner of methods to improve my growth, from eating raw liver to hanging upside down several hours a day. None of these remedies worked, of course. But I did whatever my mother asked me to do, so she wouldn't be ashamed of me.

On Sundays, she took me to church. Few from the circus attended church—few in Paris for that matter. My father never accompanied us and scowled with derision when my mother put the veil on her head and led me out the door. We always sat in the darkest row in the back. I would watch my mother pray, often with tears in her eyes, her hands clasped together in what seemed like desperation.

I didn't like going to church—it was dull and pointless compared to the thrill of the circus. But there was something else that bothered me—a sense of oppression that came over me whenever I stepped in the door, as if I were not welcome there.

Sometimes my mother went into a little closet after the Mass to speak to the priest. I waited in the pew, watching the old ladies gather hymnals. My skin would itch with the discomfort of sitting there alone. I felt the women's eyes on me with dour disapproval. Why did my mother have to talk to the priest? Perhaps she needed extra prayers or guidance in dealing with my father, whose behavior had become more and more irrational. He drank heavily and forced her to do increasingly reckless stunts, like triple flips and flying blindfolded. His own stunts were even worse—at one point he demanded that the net be removed and replaced with lit torches. The managers left him alone, not only because the trapeze act was so popular, but because they were afraid of him.

One day, I got a glimpse of why it was my father so despised me. An old man came to our house. He was tall and stooped with a dour, unpleasant face. My mother presented me to him.

"Jean-Luc, this is your great-uncle Henri."

"Hello, Uncle."

The man said nothing, just looked me over with piercing blue eyes. Then he sighed and turned away. My mother sent me to my room, but I snuck downstairs to listen to their conversation.

"It is not a condition, my dear. It is an *affliction*." The old man had a voice like sandpaper on rotted wood. "A dire secret of our family. I only wish I had known sooner, I might have prevented this."

"What can I do?"

"You must end it, before it becomes strong enough to preserve itself."

"It?" My mother gasped. "My son is not an it."

"But I am afraid it is."

They were talking about me. I heard the soft sputters of my mother weeping. "He is beautiful. He is…perfect."

"Yes, that is how it looks now. Beautiful. Practically divine. And it will remain small for so long, it is easy to think it will stay that way. Certainly in your lifetime, it will always look like a child.

But in the end… I can show you proof, the genealogy of our family since the days of Noah."

"But neither my husband nor I…I mean, we grew in the normal way."

"Your offspring is a perfect specimen of the breed. The product of two near perfect carriers. Your marriage should not have happened. An oversight on our part. We did not know your true lineage until afterward."

"*My* lineage?"

"You knew you were adopted, didn't you?"

"Me? Adopted? That's absurd."

"I'm afraid it isn't. Listen to me, you must not allow this being to persist. It will mean destruction for thousands, the start of something that can never be undone. But I know this is difficult for you, so I will help you. I will take the… child… with me now. You will not have to worry about it anymore."

Some shuffling followed—my mother getting up from the table. "That won't be necessary. Thank you for coming so far. You have been most informative."

"Are you sure you can go through with this yourself?" The old man sounded doubtful.

"I am sure."

I shuddered. Her words were cold.

I heard them go to the door—the old man left. A moment later, my mother appeared before me. Her eyes brimmed with tears. She picked me up and held me close, her face pressed in my neck. I wrapped my arms around her, stroked her hair.

"It's okay, Mama, I understand." I did, in some corner of my mind.

She took me into the bathroom and sat me on the floor. It was the first house we'd ever lived in that had running water, though the tap was outside the front stoop. I sat still and watched her come and go, filling the tub with water. When it was full, she put me in it, fully clothed. I knew I wouldn't be taking a bath.

I shivered in the frigid water and stared at up her, waiting. She took hold of my head and pressed me down under the water. I could still see her face, rippling with the water, tears streaming down her cheeks. Air bubbles burst from my nose and mouth. I waited to die, wondering how long it would take. But then my mother let go of me. She cried out, jumped up from the tub and bolted out the door.

I climbed out of the tub, dried myself off, changed my clothes, then emptied the tub bucket by bucket. I could hear my mother crying in her room. She cried a long time.

When my father returned, my mother told him about my great uncle's visit. She accused my father of lying to her all these years, of knowing exactly what my so-called affliction was. I think it was then that my father decided to do what she couldn't.

He came into my room that very night, carrying a pillow. I didn't move. I let him come. He put his knee on the bed—the mattress creaked. His eyes glowed by the moonlight streaming in from the window.

"I'm sorry, boy."

In my memory, those were the first words he'd ever spoken to me in kindness.

"It's okay, Papa."

He pressed the pillow to my face, bearing down hard. I didn't struggle, though my lungs soon screamed with pain. I wasn't afraid, which seemed odd. I should have been.

It seemed to go on a very long time. He pressed down harder and harder, and though I had no breath, I didn't die. I heard him swear in anger. "Unnatural cretin."

Then my mother's wail. "Lucas! Stop!" The pillow lifted and I coughed and gulped air as if I were drowning. My mother gathered me in her arms as my father bellowed curses and stormed out of the house. My mother held me the rest of the night.

My father came back the next morning, very drunk. "You said yourself it has to be done." He grabbed my mother and wrenched her away from me, throwing her to the floor.

She cried out. "Jean-Luc is our child. I don't care what that man said."

My father roared and drew back his fist. I jumped up from the bed, grabbed his arm and flipped him upside down—he landed on his back and groaned.

My mother gasped. My father lay on the floor, staring at me with murder in his eyes. I stood between him and my mother. He pulled himself to his feet and raised his hand to strike me. I stood my ground. He backed away from me slowly, his eyes now filled with fear. "The curse be on your head!" He stumbled from the room.

I turned to my mother. She stroked my cheek.

"My boy," she whispered, "you've made a terrible enemy this day."

My father was determined to kill me, though he wanted it to look like an accident. He tried putting me on the trapeze, but I could swing and jump to the floor without being hurt. He cursed me over and over. One night he took me from bed and carried me to the animal cages in the bowels of the Cirque d'Hiver. He tossed me into a cage with a lion named Samson, the fiercest lion in the circus. He wept as he shut the cage door and set the padlock. "Look what you made me do," he said.

I didn't cry out or call for help. I pressed my body into a corner of the cage as the lion came over and sniffed at me. I stayed still, unafraid, which seemed to perplex him greatly. When the beast finally lunged at me, I put my hand up, palm out. He stopped and crouched on his haunches, staring at me. After a time he lay down, still watching me. I put my hand down, but he didn't lunge at me again. He yawned, settled his head between his paws, and went to sleep.

The cage boy found me in the morning, locked in with the sleeping lion. He shouted until the lion tamer himself came to see what was going on. Soon a crowd had gathered as Samson, annoyed at all their noises, snapped at anyone who went near the cage door. Finally I got up, said my goodbyes to the lion, patted his mane, and walked out.

"Samson once put me in the hospital for three months," said the lion tamer, shaking his head in disbelief. "You are very lucky he was not hungry last night."

～

After that, my mother rarely let me out of her sight. I could no longer play hide and seek with the other children or run off to visit the animals or climb up to the rafters or follow Leroy into the streets. It was worse than a cage. When she was in the ring with my father, she paid Leroy to watch over me. We played checkers or Bezique in one of the dressing rooms, and I always let him win.

We were in the middle of a game one night when my father burst in, still wearing his black costume, his face bathed in sweat from the performance. One look into his eyes, and I knew my time had come. Leroy stood to bar his way, but my father shoved the man so hard he fell against the wall and lay unconscious.

"Come with me, boy."

He grabbed me by the collar and hoisted me over his shoulder. Striding from the room, he made his way through the empty corridors, the underbelly of the circus, then out into the night through a door I'd never known existed. Dangling over his back, I peered up to see darkened shop windows, rats scurrying along the street sewers, a few people bundled in cloaks darting out of the way as my father passed by. And then other strange figures appeared—featureless, distended, shadowy. They had no faces, just mouths that gaped with maniacal shrieks.

*No! No! You cannot have him! We will not let you!*

I thought it strange that I could understand what they were saying, even though they spoke no language I had ever heard before. They wrapped their tendrils around my father to slow him down—he gasped and stumbled, but he kept going. We approached the river, glimmering in the flickering gaslights. Music from the dance halls wafted in the winter air. The shadow people multiplied, engulfing us, so I was certain we had descended to some invisible world, smothered by this darkness.

My father stepped onto the bridge. Beyond the panicked chattering of the shadow people, I heard the plodding of horses and the squeak of carriage wheels. Muffled female laughter. An accordion played. We crossed a second bridge and then I knew where we were: Notre Dame.

My father pulled me from his shoulder. He crouched down.

"Get on my back, hold tight. We are going to fly tonight." He said *we*. He and I. The two of us.

I climbed onto his back and fastened my arms around his neck. He scaled the wall of the great cathedral, leaping from sills to cornices like the acrobat he was. Reaching the buttress, he tiptoed like a tight-rope walker to the roof, me still balanced on his shoulder. He kept climbing to the roof of the transept. All I could see then was the narrow spire slicing the night sky. My father walked along the pitch of the roof to the base of the spire.

The wind took my breath away. Below, the city spread like a twinkling jewel, lamplights outlining the bridge and the riverbanks. So beautiful. But I couldn't hear the music anymore—all was silent except for the wind.

"This is for your own good," he said as he climbed up the spire to the very pinnacle. "You don't want to grow up, you don't want to know what you are. You don't want to live. You cannot live. We must do this thing. It is necessary. For your mother. For all the world. You understand?"

"Yes."

"You're going to fly, boy, like you've never flown before. You like flying, don't you?"

"Yes."

"Good. Spread your wings, boy. Spread your wings."

The wind made his cheeks ripple, plastered his hair to his face. He wheezed and coughed from the exertion and the cold. The shadow people clawed him, screamed at him—it seemed they didn't want me to die. I wanted to tell them to leave my father alone. He knew what was best. But I didn't speak.

"Are you happy now?" he shouted into the wind, the black sky above. The shadow people wailed. A great sigh burst from the bottom of his soul as he let go of the spire and leapt into the night.

For a moment we flew—as he had promised. I felt the thrill of it in my throat, my stomach. My father spread his arms wide, his body flat and straight like a diver buoyed by the wind. Lights twinkled all around us, and music too, a strange music that didn't come from the dance halls below. It was the music of the shadow people, ringing in my ears. Like laughter and weeping combined.

Then a gust of wind—was that what it was?—came up under us and blew us backward, toward the church. We slammed into the transept and slid down the steep pitch, straight into the spikes that lined the edge of the roof. My father grunted as the spikes tore into his body before he flipped over the edge and hurtled to the cobbles below.

I felt the pull of those dark shadows on the way down, encircling me, protecting me as my father slammed into the pavement. I climbed off his back and gazed in wonder at his broken body, blood oozing from his crushed head. I waited for him to wake up. But he didn't. Around me the music of the night shadows magnified, filling every corner of my mind.

I sang along.

# Chapter Three

1880-1918

My father's death was my freedom. I hate saying that, but it's true. We left Paris, left the circus forever. I would miss the circus, miss the hubbub of daily shows, the heady scent of roasted chestnuts and animal shavings permeating the air, the grandeur and excitement of the Cirque d'Hiver. My mother took me south, to the town of Saint-Émilion where her sister lived. After the vibrancy of Paris, Saint-Émilion seemed like a faded ruin, a desolate village surrounded by acres of grape vines.

We lived on the estate of a wealthy winemaker and tended the vines in exchange for rent. My aunt was also a seamstress, so my mother learned to sew. She soon began making scarves from her old costumes as well as robes and dresses she'd bought in Paris. At her sister's urging, she offered them for sale in a shop in town. They were wildly popular—people came all the way from Bordeaux to buy them.

The vintner took an interest in my mother and asked her to marry him. She consented, and soon we moved to his chateau, an ancient castle seated on a hill overlooking the town. The chateau had many underground rooms and tunnels built into the rock of the hill, the perfect playroom for a lonely boy. My mother had another child, a daughter named Noele. She was "normal"—before long we looked to be the same age. If the vintner ever wondered about that, I never heard him speak of it.

My mother would not allow me to go to school—instead, she hired a tutor, Pierre, who was also a musician. After my lessons, he would take out his guitar and teach me the popular songs of the day. I was fascinated, watching his fingers move up and down the fretboard as if they were dancing. One day I asked if I could try. He laughed and handed me the instrument. His mouth dropped open when I mimicked every note he'd played.

"You learned that just from watching me?" he said.

"Of course."

Thus began my romance with the guitar. It was one of the things that sustained me through my long, long childhood.

The other was jumping. In the freedom of the countryside, I could do what I liked. The houses were close enough together that I could climb up to the rooftops and jump from roof to roof, traversing the sky above the town. I did this mostly at night. People began complaining of thumping noises on their roofs in the night, but no one ever caught me.

The shadow people continued to plague me, though they were more annoying than frightening. They came in all shapes, sometimes smaller than a speck of dust and sometimes filling an entire room. If I closed my eyes, I could feel them near—their caresses, their vaporous breath. I accepted them as a part of my strangeness. Perhaps they gave me the ability to do things other people couldn't. Perhaps they wanted to be my friends, protecting me, like the guardian angels my mother spoke of. I had no idea what darkness they awakened in me until it rose up to take control.

I learned this one day when I was walking into town to deliver my mother's newly made scarves to *La Mercerie*. I preferred to walk rather than take the carriage, because I always had an excess of energy, and it was the only time my mother let me go anywhere unaccompanied. The weather was warm, the sun shining. I took the long way around, up and down Saint-Émilion's cramped, crooked streets, sometimes jumping and flipping off walls and cartwheeling over fences. All around me, women sang as they swept their stoops, men argued while drinking tiny cups of coffee, and children played with sticks and balls.

I stopped to watch a group of bigger boys playing kickball and longed to join in. The shadow people laughed as if they knew my thoughts.

*Don't bother with them. They're stupid. Play with us! Who needs those stupid humans?*

As I stood there watching, wondering what to do, the ball flew over a boy's head and landed at my feet. I dropped the scarves and picked it up. The boys began to taunt me.

"Come on then, pipsqueak! Give it back."

*Don't give it back! Keep it. Show those stupid boys a thing or two.* The shadow people chanted.

I held the ball to my chest while they crowded around me, yelling and trying to grab the ball from my hands. I held on tight. Finally, the biggest of them drew back his fist to punch me. I ducked under his arm, dropped the ball and kicked it as hard as I could. It sailed over a nearby house and disappeared.

At first, the other boys merely stared, shocked that such a small child could kick a ball so far. Then they were angry. The big boy shoved me down. I got up and returned the shove. He sprawled on his back, the wind knocked out of him. Another boy came forward to grab me, shouting obscenities. I rammed my fist into his stomach. He doubled over with such a look of surprise on his reddening face that I laughed. The shadow people laughed too, and their laughter encouraged me. Another boy tried to tackle me. I slipped out of his grasp, swung my foot around to trip him. He did a full flip in the air before landing on his behind.

"Get him!"

They all came at me at once. I didn't try fighting back—I couldn't take them all on at once. So I lay on the ground while they kicked me and punched me and stomped on me. The strange thing was, I didn't mind the beating at all. I almost welcomed it. To feel something—anything, even pain—was better than the 'nothing' I usually felt.

Then I heard a whistle and a man's voice shouting. "Stop this at once!" The local *gendarme*— whom everyone called Monsieur Poulet, but not to his face—peeled the pile of boys off me and pulled me to my feet.

"Are you all right?"

I was covered in blood and dirt. And I was laughing.

The boys told Poulet how I had started it all by refusing to give up their ball and then kicking it over the top of the houses. But the gendarme looked at them, and then at me, a child who appeared no more than five years old, and told the boys they should stop lying and leave little children alone. He called them bullies and sent them home.

I picked up the scarves and went to the shop. The shop owner complained they were filthy, and that I was filthy, and to tell my mother never to send me again. I went home and snuck in my window so no one in my family would see me. I washed off the blood and dirt in the sink and looked in the mirror. To my amazement, I saw that the cuts and bruises on my face and arms were almost healed. In a matter of minutes.

I continued to take the scarves into town, despite the shopkeeper's objections. I also delivered wine to local estates and restaurants. Sometimes grown men would try to steal the goods, but I'd give them a thrashing and they would leave me alone. If the town boys provoked me, I reacted swiftly and violently, spurred on by the shadow people. Something would come over me, a heat from deep inside, bursting through my skin.

When I sent a boy to the hospital with a broken arm, M. Poulet had had enough. He dragged me to my mother with a dire warning to keep me away from the village. My mother was horrified and forbade me to leave the grounds of the chateau. But that didn't matter to me. I simply jumped out my third-story bedroom window whenever I wanted to wander. I took care to stay away from the town during the day, only going out at night, prowling the rooftops. The shadow people took great delight in my midnight outings. They became my only companions, whispering to me, urging me to do things I didn't want to do.

*See that old woman? What would it take to knock her down, take her purse? Hardly anything. You are stronger. You are more deserving. Go on. Do it.*

*Look! That mean old shopkeeper left his door wide open. He sleeps in the back room. Someone ought to teach him a lesson.*

*Remember the boy who punched you? You could climb into his window and show him who is boss. Watch his eyes as the life drains away. There is nothing like it.*

The only thing that quelled the chattering of the shadow people was music. At Pierre's suggestion, my mother bought me a guitar, and I played for hours every day. I learned the works of the great guitar masters of the Romantic period, Giuliani and Sor. But it was the compositions of the French guitarist Napoléon Coste that captivated me for their sheer beauty and haunting melancholy. I soon began making up my own songs, though I never played those for Pierre—he would think them childish and silly.

Pierre told my mother he had never seen a talent such as a mine, that I was a prodigy and should go to the conservatory in Bordeaux. I had a great future in music ahead of me. My mother refused, no matter how often Pierre begged her. She would not hear of me going anywhere away from her. "He's far too young." This was a lie, but it didn't matter. I didn't want to go to the conservatory—didn't want to perform for anyone. I only wanted—needed—the music. To keep the shadow people quiet.

~

Time passed slowly. My sister Noele grew up and married the winery manager. She had two children—a daughter, Colette, and a son, Raphael. They became my new siblings. The twentieth century had begun, though I barely knew it. Little had changed in Saint-Émilion, though automobiles began to replace horses and a few modern people even installed electricity in their homes. My family spurned the modern world—they preferred the old ways.

My life went on as it always had…an unending childhood. Colette and Raphael grew to be my size, though neither of them seemed to think this was strange. It was nice have friends to play with, even though Noele did her best to keep her children away from me.

One night, Raphael's father brought home a gift for his son's birthday, the newly published novel *Peter Pan*. After he'd read aloud the first couple of chapters, Raphael turned to me and said, "Jean-Luc! This is a story about you!"

A boy who can fly, who never grows up, who is followed by a shadow and who adopts real children as his playmates. All I was missing was Tinkerbell. I thrilled to the story, looking forward to the reading each night, especially when Peter and the children went to Neverland. Raphael begged me to take him to Neverland—he seemed certain that's where I had come from. Something about the idea of Neverland made me long for it, yearn for it, as I'd never wanted anything in my life. I promised him I would take him there, one day.

Ten years later the war came, a war like nothing the world had seen before. A world war, engulfing all of Europe. We did not pay that much attention at first. The front was far from us, and demand for wine increased markedly—my family prospered. But then Noele's husband was conscripted. He assured her that he would not be going to the front—men over thirty were usually given administrative duties.

"Don't worry. The war will be short. I will be back within the year."

But he didn't come back. The war soon became a catastrophe. We heard statistics too horrific to be believed: Two hundred thousand killed or wounded at the Battle of Marne. Ninety thousand lost at Champagne, sixty-six thousand at the Somme. France lost so many men it was forced to deploy nearly every able-bodied man to the Western Front, regardless of age. Noele's husband went in 1916. He died at the Battle of Verdun.

Raphael was seventeen at the time. He knew he would be conscripted as soon as he reached eighteen, so he made preparations. He married the girl he'd been courting and they immediately had a child—many men were doing that, to make sure their line would continue. They named the boy Raphael II. When little Rafe, as we called him, was a year old, Raphael left for the front. He was killed during the German spring offensive of 1918, in a battle presciently called Operation Michael. The funeral was held on a dreary day in April, its images burned forever into my memories. The black-draped coffin, my sister's grief at the loss of her only son in addition to her husband. Gazing at the awful, sad scene, I thought of Peter Pan and Neverland, and wondered if Raphael would get there before me.

What I felt was neither grief nor sorrow, but a mere widening of the void that always existed inside me. With every death, every loss, the emptiness grew. I tried to fill it with music, but that was a temporary fix. I tried God as well. I went to church faithfully. I read the Bible over and over. Yet God seemed so distant. I never felt Him move within me as my mother had. God was not a father to me, He was a judge. He had the face of my earthly father, the one who wanted me dead.

Shortly after Raphael's death, my mother became ill. Within weeks, she was bedridden. Doctors and priests came and went. Noele sat by her bed each night, crying. I spied her through the crack in the doorway, but I never went in. I didn't want to see my beautiful mother die.

Finally, she summoned me to her bedside. I hardly recognized her. Her nearly eighty years of living—never obvious in her appearance until now—made themselves keenly visible in every wrinkle, every curve of her cheek and chin. Gray, milky eyes. Skin dry as parchment. My beautiful mother had begun to resemble the shadow people that haunting my waking life.

She took my hand and gripped it hard. "Jean-Luc," she whispered. "I love you."

No one had ever said those words to me.

"You know that you are special. Different. That is not a fault of yours. But still, you must be careful. Stay hidden. Keep away from the world. Don't let them see you. Because they will want to…use you."

"Use me? For what?"

She didn't answer that question. "You must never marry," she said. "Never take a wife. Have nothing to do with women. Ever. That is very important. You must promise."

I promised. She sighed, as if in relief. "You will have a long life, Jean-Luc. Live as best you can. I know you are good, deep inside. You can be good. You can resist the thing that is inside of you. I have prayed for you every day—that God would have mercy on you."

She let out a long breath and did not take another one. Her face relaxed, her eyes closed. She looked tranquil, at peace. Her hand slipped from mine.

I had never imagined life without my mother. What would I do? I was still a child in the world's eyes. I was Peter Pan, the boy who would never grow up. I thought about killing myself then, so I could go to Neverland, be with her, with Raphael, forever. Neverland and Heaven were the same to me.

My sister Noele became my new "mother." She decided to

make a new start, especially since people in town were starting to ask uncomfortable questions about me. After the war, she sold the winery and we moved again, to a smaller wine estate in Bordeaux. At once ancient and timeless, Bordeaux was at that time considered the most beautiful city in France outside of Paris. What pleased me most was that the city had many more rooftops than Saint-Émilion. I spent my days in the fields, tending vines with Rafe and the workers or playing guitar, and my nights prowling the roofs of the city, leaping and dancing with the shadow people.

And so passed another twenty years.

Until 1938, when my world changed forever.

# Chapter Four

## 1938-1945

Colette tossed a newspaper on the breakfast table. In blaring letters the headline screamed, *"Attaché dead. Nazis riot and fire synagogues."* From my seat at the table, I read the first few lines of the article.

Nazis, enraged at the assassination in Paris by a young Polish Jew of Ernest von Rath, minor German diplomat, early today retaliated by smashing windows of all Jewish stores...

"They are calling it the *Kristallnacht.*" Colette sank into a chair, visibly shaking, her face white as a sheet. "Nearly a hundred Jews killed, four hundred Jewish shops sacked, synagogues burned..."

"What has this to do with us?" Noele buttered her toast, barely looking at the paper. "We are not Jewish. And we are far from Germany."

"We are not Jewish. We are something worse." She turned her gaze on me. "*He* is something worse."

"Come now, what does Jean-Luc have to do with this?"

"I have had my eye on this Adolf Hitler." Colette leaned toward her mother and lowered her voice, as if about to reveal a terrible secret. "He was raised to power by a secret organization called the Thule Society—they believe in a master race, descended from gods who live deep in the earth. They believe that their leader, Baldyr, is their messiah, the one who will release them and give them dominion over the earth."

"So they are idiots. What of it?"

"Do you not understand? They are looking for him." Again, she pointed to me.

"Nonsense." Noele set down her knife. "They are certainly not coming all the way to our corner of the world looking for a little boy."

"Little boy? What a laugh. Anyway, how do you know? They have spies, researchers, people who know where to look. They will search to the ends of the earth. *Maman*, we must take him out of France."

"Don't be ridiculous. We are not leaving. Jean-Luc is perfectly safe here."

"And if they come for him?"

"God will not allow it."

They did not speak of this again, in my hearing. Our lives went on as usual, despite the rise of the Nazis in Germany. We French had no fear of the Germans—we'd conquered them before, we would do it again.

Then Germany invaded Poland, and France began sending soldiers to the Maginot Line. Colette renewed her quest to leave the country. Noele steadfastly refused, saying she was almost seventy, too old to move anywhere.

"Take him, if you must. And Rafe too. Leave me here to die alone."

Frustrated, Colette gave up the idea of leaving France. And for a time, it seemed her fears were unfounded. France and Germany faced each other on the western front for over a year in what became known as the Phony War. The French papers said Germany would eventually back down—even Hitler did not want another world war.

But then Hitler invaded Norway.

"Look at this!" Colette slammed yet another newspaper on the kitchen table. This one bore the headline: *Oslo Falls to Germans.* "Do you see now?" She faced her mother with steely determination. "Why would Germany invade Norway, a neutral country? It is because that is where they are said to come from!"

Noele didn't pause from peeling potatoes to look at the paper.

"No one invades a country because of fairy tales about divine giants. That would be preposterous."

"These Nazis *are* preposterous," Colette retorted. "They believe completely in their divine right to rule the world. And they believe they will find their messiah."

"I thought Hitler *was* their messiah!" Noele picked up another potato. Neither of them acknowledged me, eating a soft-boiled egg at the table.

Colette paced the kitchen, wringing her hands. "What about Rafe? He is of age for the draft. Do you want to lose him as you lost your husband and son? He is your only grandson. If he dies…" She didn't finish.

Noele's peeling knife stilled.

"Mama." Colette sank into a chair and set her hands flat on the table. "We can go to Canada. A new beginning."

Noele shook her head. "I am too old for new beginnings."

Colette straightened. "Then I will go without you."

Her mother said nothing.

There were no passenger ships sailing out of France, so Colette booked passage on a freighter from Bordeaux to Halifax. Her friends thought she was crazy. Bordeaux was immune to war. The wine business always thrived in war time. And Hitler, they insisted, would never invade France. The Germans had tried that in the first war and failed miserably. France boasted a superior army and had built an immutable defense at the Maginot Line. Hitler possessed neither the strength nor the spine to cross it.

They were wrong, of course.

We left from the port of Bordeaux a week later, in late May of 1940, two weeks before the Germans stormed into Paris. The freighter carried only twelve passengers. Rafe and I slept on the floor in the dank, cramped cabin while Colette had the narrow bed, though I don't think she slept a single night on board that ship. I enjoyed the journey—the cold sea air, the lack of rules. I did not have to be hidden from anyone. We ate our meals with the crew who enthralled me with their licentious stories and hardened ways, so different from the men I'd known in my life.

By the time we landed in Halifax, we learned that Germany had overrun France in a matter of days. They occupied the entire western coast, including Bordeaux.

Colette sent a telegram to her mother, begging for news. We stayed in a boarding house in Halifax for a month while she waited for a reply. Finally, we received a brief letter which showed clear signs of having been opened and resealed several times. The Germans had occupied Noele's estate and were "drinking all the wine." Most of the rest was blacked out.

"She will be fine," Rafe said, words of comfort for his aunt. "After the war, we will go back."

"Yes, of course," said Colette.

But we didn't.

Halifax was overcrowded, filthy and jammed with drunken servicemen—a far cry from Bordeaux. We traveled farther west, and Colette bought a small, neglected vineyard on the Niagara Escarpment. The property included a two-story farmhouse with gaps in the slat floors and cracks in the walls, a far cry from our stately house in Bordeaux.

Still concerned that I would be "discovered," Colette changed my name to Jared. She even managed to get me a forged birth certificate and a passport.

"Why Jared?" I asked her.

"It is an appropriate name." But she never explained why this was.

I had learned not to ask questions. Colette was a hard woman, as Noele had been. They were warriors, and I was their battleground. To protect me and to protect their progeny *from* me was their primary goal. I was an unbearable burden, a tragic flaw, a fearful secret they spent their lives trying to keep from the world.

Rafe, Colette and I worked round the clock and brought the vineyard back to life. Winters in Niagara were long and harsh, but late springs and mild summers produced a dark, fruity wine similar to the Burgundy back home. We spent summers in the field and winters turning the old barn and silos into a wine-processing operation. Within a few years we were sending bottles to market. The quality nowhere matched that of our Bordeaux wines, but the Canadians seemed not to mind.

We watched the war unfold from a distance, the mounting horrors, the madness that seemed beyond the scope of human imagination. Stories came of the suffering of the French under occupation. A part of me thought they deserved it. France had been arrogant and cowardly. The French army had dallied too long, allowing Hitler to reform his battle plan, build up his forces and overrun them. Paris had surrendered without a fight. All to save precious monuments. The French cared more about their art and architecture than their people.

We heard nothing from Noele in all that time. Either she didn't bother to write, or her letters were intercepted. Colette wrote faithfully every week, without knowing if her letters reached her mother. We would have to wait until the war was over.

Germany was defeated, in the end. The Nazis never found their messiah, Baldyr. They never found the gods who would give them dominion of the world. Noele was right, perhaps: God would not allow it. And yet God had allowed unspeakable devastation—millions dead, extermination camps, whole cities plowed under. Generations lost forever.

Shortly after France was liberated, Colette received a letter from the French government. They had recovered our estate from the retreating Germans, but Noele was dead. She'd suffered a heart attack just weeks after the occupation began. The German commandant had seen to the burial but never informed the French provisional government in Vichy.

Colette didn't believe the heart attack story. She believed her mother had committed suicide rather than submit to the Germans. Perhaps I should have been sad, but in truth I didn't feel much of anything. Colette was stoic, as always. Rafe seethed with anger, but there was no vent for his emotion, no way to seek retribution. We heard a wealthy Spaniard bought the estate for a fraction of its true worth. After the taxes were paid—for the government still insisted on collecting taxes for all the years the Germans occupied the land—Colette received the proceeds.

Rafe went off to agricultural college in Toronto. He returned two years later and took over the running of the winery. By then I looked to be about thirteen years old. And miracle of miracles, I had grown tall, nearly as tall as Rafe. My strength proved an asset—I could do the work of four men without tiring. Rafe put me in charge of the vineyards and focused his own efforts on winemaking. The work kept me busy and the shadow people at bay. In the evenings I played my guitar under the night sky or went to the escarpment to jump. I felt free and happy in those times. Alive for over eighty years, I was just becoming a teenager. And then Rafe decided that I should go to school.

# Chapter Five

1955

"It's an all-boys academy with an excellent music program." Rafe set before Colette a rumpled brochure. Under a large green crest were the words *Saint James School for Boys* and the motto: *Men of Character from Boys of Promise*. "Just outside Toronto."

"Toronto! That's so far away!"

"Only an hour by rail. Besides, it's a boarding school. He will live there during the school year."

Colette picked up the brochure, browsed it quickly and set it down again. "He's never lived away from home. It could be—dangerous."

"We are past all that."

"His mother would not approve."

"His mother is dead. It is a new world now. We must move forward. *Jared* must move forward. He can't remain a child forever. *Tante*, it is time the boy went to school. Had a normal life."

"What about his life is normal?"

"He's no different from any other boy in most ways. And he must improve his English. Lose his accent. He can't do that being alone all day working in the fields or skulking in his room. He needs friends. Companions. He needs socialization."

"You don't remember what happened the last time he tried to

socialize." Bitterness soured Colette's voice.

"I've already spoken to the headmaster. He understands that Jared has some…quirks."

Colette's eyebrow shot up as she regarded her nephew. "And what will they think when the other boys start to age and he doesn't?"

"He is tall for his age," Rafe said. "It will not be an issue for a few years. And if it becomes one, we will withdraw him."

"What about his chores? He does over half the farm work himself."

"He can work in the summer. He'll go to school only in the winter."

Colette gave up arguing. In truth, I think she wanted to get rid of me. Winters were long enough without the daily reminder of my presence.

Rafe and I took the train to Toronto to tour the school and meet with the headmaster. He told me to be on my best behavior and to "act like a real thirteen-year-old."

"He will interview you, ask you questions. Don't say anything more than necessary. You're shy. Introverted. Your English is not very good. Stick with that."

We took a cab to an imposing, stone manor house surrounded by lush lawns and gardens. A fountain gushed in the center of the drive. The school reminded me fondly of the venerable estates of Bordeaux.

The headmaster, Mr. Lewis, greeted us at the entrance. Tall and trim, he sported a graying pompadour and black-rimmed glasses.

"Well, young man, it is nice to meet you." He put his hand out to shake. No one had ever done this to me before. Rafe nudged me and I placed my hand into a solid, firm grip. "Jared, is it? So you are from France."

"Yes."

"Then I don't suppose I need to sign you up for French class." Mr. Lewis snickered at his own joke. "But if you need extra help with English, we will provide you a tutor. And I understand you are interested in music?"

"Yes."

"He's quite an accomplished guitar player." Rafe seemed eager to please Mr. Lewis.

"Well, that is excellent. Unfortunately, our music programs do not include the guitar. But one of our professors has a small jazz band that meets after school. Perhaps that would interest you?"

I perked up at the word "jazz." Back in Bordeaux, Noele used to tune in to Duke Ellington and Dizzy Gillespie on her radio. At the time, such music was a kind of antidote to the looming war—uplifting and somewhat rebellious.

"Yes," I said again.

"Good. We'll meet up with him later so he can hear you play." Mr. Lewis jotted something down on his ledger. He then explained the curriculum and the expectations. I was issued a uniform for school and a separate one for gym class. "We have many sports programs—do you like sports?"

"I like jumping—"

"He's not really a sports type." Rafe's voice held an edge of nervousness. He didn't want me displaying my abilities in front of the other kids and didn't trust me to fake it.

"Jumping, did you say?" said Mr. Lewis. "Perhaps track and field is the place for you. We do require all our students to participate in one sport. It's part of creating a well-rounded person. You will meet lots of your friends that way. Would that suit?"

Mr. Lewis' pen hung poised over the ledger, ready to write. I nodded. Rafe sucked in a breath.

"Very good!" The headmaster scribbled. "Well then, let me give you a tour and show you the dormitory where you will be living, and then you can have lunch with some of the students. Get to know everyone."

Rafe and I followed Mr. Lewis up and down halls and stairways, peeking into classrooms where dull-eyed students gazed at us with guarded interest. The dormitory lacked any kind of cheer, but at least the students could put posters on the walls. After the tour, Mr. Lewis ushered us into a cavernous dining room, where huge banners displaying the school crest hung between massive stone columns. Old tapestries depicting ancient wars lined the walls. Mr. Lewis instructed me to sit at the table with a group of boys "my age," and then took Rafe off to sit at the faculty table.

"Hello." My French accent whittled the greeting to "allo."

"You sound funny." A boy with sandy hair and blotches of

freckles spoke first. "Where are you from?"

"Uh…France."

"France? You're French?" All the boys giggled. "Wee wee Mon-soor! Bon Joor! Common tally voo?" They took turns mangling every French word they knew, which was thankfully not many.

"I'm Findlay." A smallish boy with glasses put his hand out over the table. He was the only one not laughing. "Sixth grade."

"Jared," I said.

"We go by last names here."

"Oh…Laurent."

The boys laughed again, holding their noses as they repeated my name.

"What grade you in, Lore?" asked Findlay, mispronouncing my name.

"Uh…I do not know."

"How old are you?"

"Thirteen."

"Seventh or eighth then," said Findlay.

"He'll have to go back to fifth, since he don't hardly speak English." The freckled boy's comment brought on more laughter.

"He speaks better than you, Beggars," said Findlay. "'Don't hardly speak English?' What language is that?"

Beggars' face reddened at the other boys' continued merriment, and he scowled.

Just then a waiter rolled a trolley up to our table and set plates before us. Another waiter filled glasses.

Findlay peppered me with questions throughout the meal of meatloaf and green beans. He continued to call me "Lore" and I didn't correct him. I rather liked the name. I gave him the cover story Colette and Rafe had established for me: my father and I had emigrated from southern France the year before to help care for my aging grandmother. My mother was dead. I was an only child.

"How did your mom die?"

"Tuberculosis." It was common enough.

"Do you have it too? Are you going to give us some French disease?" another boy asked, to a fresh wave of snickers.

The shadow people descended. *Show them. Teach them who you are. Put the little cockroaches in their place.* I started to hum to myself. I'd found that humming alleviated the pressure of the shadow people to some extent. The boys found it funny.

"I guess he didn't understand you." Beggars cleared his throat and then spoke loudly and slowly, as if I were deaf. "Do you have a French disease?"

I shook my head and squeezed my eyes shut, breathing against the murmurs that turned to roars in my ears. *Show them! Show them! Show them!*

"How are you boys getting on?" Cheerful Mr. Lewis appeared, saving me.

"Very well, Headmaster." The boys spoke in unison.

"I hope you will make Jared feel welcome. He's come a long way to be here with us."

They all nodded and smiled and offered words of assurance. The boys clearly liked their headmaster, or at least respected him.

"If you're finished, Jared, I'd like you meet Mr. Holiday, the jazz band director."

Grateful, I excused myself and followed Mr. Lewis to the faculty lunch table. A young man with wild orange hair jumped up, grabbed my hand and shook it violently.

"The guitarist? Finally! My prayers have been answered! Tell me, are you any good?"

"Well, I have never played jazz—"

"He is a very quick learner." Rafe winked at me.

"Brilliant! Come with me. Call me Holiday, by the way. Everyone does. I don't care for all that mister nonsense." Still holding my hand, he dragged me from the dining hall through a long corridor and into a large room crammed with musical instruments. He rifled through a closet, pulled out a guitar case and set it carefully on the floor. With near-reverence, he raised the lid and lifted up a guitar unlike any I'd ever seen before. Two scroll-like sound holes rather than one large one graced the center of the instrument. There was a round knob at the bottom.

"Have you played one of these before?"

I shook my head.

He took out a long cord and plugged it into the base of the guitar, the other end into a speaker-like box. I jumped at the unexpected loud, popping noise.

"It always does that." Mr. Holiday plucked a few strings—the sound was bold and muscular and electric. A shock to the senses. "Want to give it a try?" I hesitated, not sure what to do with the thing. "Go on. Play something."

I took the guitar onto my lap. It felt awkward, sleeker and yet heavier than my old guitar. I was afraid to even touch the strings.

"Um…can you play…a recording?" I asked. "Of what you like."

"What? Oh! Certainly." He jumped up, sped over to a cluttered shelf and pulled out a record album. He slipped it from the cover and put it on a turntable. "This is Al Casey. He's one of my favorites."

What ascended from the scratchy disc was a revelation—music that seemed created for joy, for dancing. My heart quickened, my fingers tapped the top of the guitar in rhythm. This was not the plodding, languid jazz of France or even of Canada. This music was wholly American.

Holiday snapped his fingers and bobbed his head. Totally gawky. "Like it?"

I nodded. Within a few minutes I was playing along, copying the melody I heard. The strings reverberated under my fingers in a way I found intoxicating. The shadow people screamed, but their cries were distant. Suddenly the track ended, leaving only the scratches and pops of the vinyl. I stopped playing and glanced at the turntable, wondering why Holiday didn't pick up the needle. He was staring at me in slack-jawed wonder.

"You say you've never played jazz before?"

I shook my head. "I pick up quick."

"Indeed." A huge smile cracked his face in half. "Well, then, Jared my boy, welcome to Saint James School Jazz Band. Please stay forever."

I grinned back. I just might.

# Chapter Six

1960

Shortly after I started school, Rafe got married. I suspected this was the real reason he had pushed Colette into sending me away. I returned home the following summer to find my room transformed into a nursery. I was moved to a lower back room of the house nearer the servants quarters. That was fine with me—I hardly slept anyway. Besides, I was so grateful to Rafe for sending me to school in the first place, I would forgive him anything.

Saint James was the perfect place for me. Though I had my struggles fitting in and "acting the part" of a preteen, I had found my first real friends in Holiday and the other members of the jazz band—Findlay in particular, who played the trombone. They were mostly misfits like me, devoted to a kind of music that was not at all fashionable in their age group, and to an overly excitable teacher who seemed at any moment on the brink of bursting at the seams. I poured my soul into jazz band. I listened to every recording I could get my hands on until I could play it note for note. After a few months, I could make up my own riffs with ease. Jazz felt like the most natural kind of music in the world, a music built to conform to the human soul. The shadow people hated it. Which made me love it all the more.

Now it was the day of graduation, and I was genuinely sorry

to be leaving the school. My age, or lack thereof, had become noticeable and worrisome two years ago, but I begged Rafe to let me stay. I cut my hair and lifted weights to build up muscle so I would look older. I even dusted my chin with dirt to give the appearance of a beard.

I had done well in school. I now spoke English like a native Canadian and had read nearly every book in the library. I had participated in the long jump but dutifully kept to the middle of the pack, occasionally winning an event to show I was trying. The shadow people came to me less and less. Relieved beyond measure, I was careful to avoid people or situations that might awaken them.

I managed to maintain my distance and yet stay friendly with most of the boys. Holiday proved more difficult. The only person who seemed genuinely interested in me, his probing questions were often difficult to avoid.

"So were your parents musicians?"

"Not that I know of."

"What about your grandparents?"

"They were in the circus."

"The circus! Intriguing! Do you remember seeing them perform?"

"Not really."

"Too bad. And what does your father do?"

"He runs a winery." Surely Holiday knew this already—he'd met Rafe on several occasions.

"Yes, yes, but tell me…is he really your father? I'm only wondering because he seems a little young, and you told me he just married a couple of years ago…look, I don't mean to pry. But quite often there's a reason some boys are sent off to boarding school."

I didn't offer an explanation. I figured I would start getting caught up in lies and make a mess of it. I let him think whatever he wanted. He would never guess the truth.

Graduation was held in the school chapel—a small ceremony, only forty boys in the class. When my name was called there was little applause, as no one from my family had come. Colette didn't like to travel, and Rafe was busy with the winery. Mr. Lewis shook my hand and smiled benignly as he handed me the diploma—I don't think he even remembered me. Holiday was beside himself, practically weeping. He begged me to return to the school as a teacher one day. He'd been disappointed that I had no plans for college. I told him I was needed at home.

After the ceremony, Findlay shook my hand. He'd grown four inches since our first meeting—he was taller than me. His pudginess was mostly gone, as were his glasses. He'd turned into a man, while I remained a child.

"Keep in touch, mate," he said. "Come and visit. I'll still be here another year, if they don't throw me out."

"Why would they?" But I knew. Like most of the boys, Findlay had been caught more than once with alcohol in his room. He was always on probation. Alcohol was the one thing all the boys had in common. Findlay had tried time and again to get me to join in, but I steadfastly refused.

"You must be one of those Mormons," he had said with a laugh after the tenth time I turned down his offer.

"Something like that."

~

I went home to Niagara. Rafe and his wife Monique welcomed me with chilly politeness. Colette, now in her late fifties, greeted me with indifference. Little Raphael the Third was another matter. Now four years old and bright for his age, he filled that big, silent house with glorious sound. He talked constantly, asking an endless stream of questions without ever waiting for the answers. The moment I came in the door, he grabbed hold of my hand and screamed to the world, "My big brother is home!"

Big brother—something I had never been before. Ralph followed me into the fields each day, asking a million questions and hardly ever waiting for an answer. I taught him how to trim and train the vines, pick the grape clusters, and fertilize the soil. I had him hoe weeds and set traps for gophers. Having him there injected some fun into my life—the days went by faster. Sometimes on warm days we went fishing down at the Twenty River or we climbed the escarpment to see the view from the ridge. I took him to the falls, delighting in his gleeful laughter as the spray from the mighty waters soaked us to the skin. We even went to the circus when Barnum and Bailey came to Niagara in the summer. Ralph loved the circus as much as I did, though it proved much-changed from the circus I remembered, nearly a century before.

"Our great grandmother flew on the trapeze," I told him.

"No! Really? Do we have any pictures?"

"I don't think so." Any pictures that might have existed were lost or buried in a trunk somewhere in the old house in Bordeaux. Colette brought little with her when we left France.

"Have you ever swung on the trapeze?" he asked me.

"Yes, once. I tried it."

"What was it like?"

"Like—flying."

"Show me."

I hesitated. I shouldn't do it. But the tree under which we sat had a long, sturdy branch, so I showed him how I would swing, flinging my body all the way around and flying off, landing on my feet. He clapped and wanted to try, so I lifted him to the branch and gave him a rudimentary lesson. But as soon as I let go, he screamed to be let down.

"I think I'll be a clown," he said with a laugh.

"You'd make a good clown."

*Jared.*

A voice, soft and insistent. It usually happened in those brief silences.

*Come to me.*

This voice was different from the shadow people. Alluring…mysterious—it made me want to obey. Sometimes I answered.

*I don't know where you are.*

*You do. You do. Follow your heart.*

*Who are you?*

*You already know.*

I hummed to myself.

"What are you humming?" Ralph gave me a curious look.

"I don't know. Something I've heard."

"It's pretty. You should write a song."

I've written many songs, though no one has heard them but me.

~

When Ralph wasn't with me, I filled my mind with other things. Music or work or reading or jumping. I kept a list of things I would do when I finally grew up. Sail around the world. Climb Mount Everest (I was pretty sure I could do that without any special gear.) Go deep sea diving. Jump off Victoria's Falls. Maybe I would finally join the circus. I could be the greatest trapeze artist who ever lived.

And yet I knew I would do none of these things.

*Why not?* said the Voice. *With your abilities, you could conquer the world. You are mine, Jared. You are my blood. The greatest of all.*

*No.* Each time I said the word, it became less convincing.

The Voice would chuckle indulgently. *We will see about that.*

# Chapter Seven

1972

Ralph grew up.

He went to school—not Saint James but a local school, so he could live at home. He was never interested in sports, but was very smart and was taking high school courses by the time he reached junior high. He made new friends and had sleepovers at their houses and went to camp and later on to concerts and furtive gatherings in other people's basements. He wore tie-dyed shirts and grew his hair long and disdained our old-fashioned ways. He left me behind, attracted to his new crowd, new experiences.

When he was home, he spent most of his time in his room, record player blaring loud, angry music that bled through the heavy oak doors of the house. The shadow people stirred within me, their voices screeching in my ears like the feedback of a faulty speaker. For the first time in my long life, music made me afraid.

I tried to stay away, but the heavy bass beat that shook the floorboards drew me in. I stood outside Ralph's door, my ear pressed to the oak. The shadow people sang and danced around me with unfettered joy. The Voice laughed and coaxed.

*Dance, child.*

I danced. Ralph would tell me to go away, shut the door in my face. But I couldn't stop. Whenever it played, I would go to his room. If he locked the door, I broke the doorknob to get in. Blood pulsed in my ears, behind my eyes. My body felt like liquid iron, hot and fiery. I became something else, some other creature, not human and not animal, cloaked in the shadow people so that the door, the landing, the house itself disappeared.

Then one day, I found myself sprawled on my back on the front lawn, covered in shattered glass. Ralph was bent over me, his eyes wide with terror.

"What happened?" I asked.

"You jumped through the window." Ralph's voice shook. "*Right through the glass*. What were you doing?"

"I was…dancing."

Ralph shook his head. "You're sick, Jared. Sick."

I sat up. Tiny shards of glass were embedded in my arms. Blood covered my hands and trickled down my face, warm and sticky. Yet I felt no pain.

"You need to get to a hospital."

"I'll be fine." I jumped to my feet and ran away ran to the barn where I could wash in the animal trough.

Ralph followed me. "What's going on with you?"

"Nothing. Go away. I'm fine." I didn't want him to see me. But he spun me around and stared at me. His mouth dropped open.

"Your face…a minute ago it was all cut up."

"No, it was just the blood. I washed it off."

"What are you, Jared?"

The question stopped me cold. "What do you mean?"

"Come on, man. There's something wrong with you. Everyone tiptoes around you. No one wants to talk. My father says you're just different. But you aren't just different. You're like…an *alien*."

The way he said it, the look in his eyes, horror mixed with revulsion—his words burrowed like a knife into my heart.

"It was…the music," I whispered. "It made me…dance."

"You call that dancing?" He laughed, sharp, cutting. "Then stay away from my room. Better yet, stay away from me." He turned his back and walked out of the barn.

*Stay away.*

I knew then that I had to leave. This house, this family. I would have to find my own way in a world I didn't know. A world that could never learn what I really was.

~

I left that night. Better in the night, when I was usually awake and the family slept. The house lay in darkness but for the flickering light and muffled, tin-can sounds coming from the housekeeper's sitting room down the hall—Rhianne often stayed up late watching television and drinking Cointreau.

I crept out a back door, shouldering my old school backpack and my guitar, and headed down the hill toward the grapevines—a last visit, one final stroll through the vines that had become like children to me through the years. I'd even given them names and would sometimes talk to them, coaxing the stragglers and rewarding healthy fruit-bearers. A game of sorts, but also a sad statement of my loneliness. *He talks to the plants because he has no friends.*

I thought of my mother. Charmaine. She had loved me. She had prayed for me every day of her life. She had protected me from my father and from the world. I had made a promise to her that I would stay hidden from the world, and I meant to keep it.

Besides, there was no one left. Little Ralph had loved me for a time, but no longer. I was truly alone, and that was fine. I could deal with that, accept it. Much easier than striving for love. The world, I guessed, was a loveless place. It suited me better.

I walked. West, away from the lakes and into the prairie, where only barns, grain elevators and tall, silver silos disrupted the rolling landscape of barley and wheat fields. I remembered my geography from school: Ontario, Manitoba, Saskatchewan, Alberta, British Columbia. The provinces looked huge and empty even on a map—I assumed it would take years to pass through them all.

I'd never seen so much space, so much sky. I stayed away from the highways, fearing some good Samaritan driver might want to give me a ride. The only sounds I heard most days were the wind bending the wheat and the rumbling of tractors in the fields. I bought food from roadside diners and drank from local streams or the occasional water pump. On those nights when I stopped to rest, I found an abandoned shed or garage—sometimes just a copse of trees, where I'd play my guitar to drown out the shadow people. I'd think of Ralph and Colette and wonder how they were doing, and if they missed me at all.

Then one day, a new danger presented itself. I stopped at a diner to buy an apple—I was pretty low on money by that time. And someone spoke to me.

"You play?"

I looked up. A teenage girl at the register gazed at me with a kind of gauzy intensity. I stood still, my hand stuck halfway in my pocket, fingers clinging to the cold quarter there. I had known few girls in my life besides those in my family. I'd gone to an all-boys school with no female teachers. This had been by design—my mother had warned me never to marry, never to take up with women. But when I looked into the eyes of this young waitress—helpless and dreamy and filled with sickening adoration, something new and treacherous awoke in the core of my being.

She repeated the question I had not answered. "Do you play?"

"What? Oh. Yeah."

"Would you play something? Apple is free. Plus your choice." She lifted the glass lid off a plate of donuts on the counter. "Please? I'd love to hear you."

*Play for the girl! Play!* The voices of the shadow people screamed at me, gleeful. Their spindly arms reached toward the girl, pulling her spirit toward me, drawing her in.

I set the quarter for the apple on the counter, spun, and ran from the diner. My heart beat like a timpani on my chest, the urge to go back so great I had to push myself forward, like I was walking into a hurricane. The shadow people screamed. And then the Voice roared in my ears.

*Go back to her.*

"No!" I screamed the word into the thick summer air. "No!" But the effort took everything from me and I dropped to my knees. The apple slipped from my hand and rolled into the dust. My whole body became a vortex of pain, twisting through my intestines to the ends of my fingers. I had not known pain before that moment. But this was not physical—it was something far worse. I crouched in the dirt a long time, panting, waiting, *hoping* it would pass.

*This is who you are. Accept. Learn to love it.*

I knew I had reached a threshold, like when the shadow people first came, when I felt the first urge to fight, to hurt, when the

Voice first began to speak. But this one seemed more perilous by far. I could no longer go into diners or anywhere I might see a girl again.

When my money ran out, I found work on ranches. Most of the ranch hands were drifters who stayed for a season and then moved on, making it easy for me to fit in. I learned to hay fields, to tend gardens, to go on long cattle drives to summer pastures. In the winter, I'd find a place where the barns needed fixing or the fences mending. People drifted in and out of my life like shadows—I rarely learned their names. The only women I met were sturdy, unsmiling rancher wives. I lost myself in the empty stillness of the prairie and played my guitar to shut out the voices.

My life had a certain rhythm to it—I knew when it was time to move, find a new place. No one asked me questions. No one cared to know anything about me. I did the work of three men for whatever the rancher was willing to pay. I avoided the comradery of the bunk houses and left when the work was done.

Sometimes in the night I would ponder this existence and wonder why I didn't just end it all. Had my father been right all along? Would I be better off dead? What kind of life was this anyway? A life without human connection. Devoid of love. My existence seemed a waste. I never really knew where I was. I just kept moving west. But what would happen when I got to the end of the road?

Ten years passed before I found out.

# PART TWO

# Revelation

After this I looked, and there before me
was a door standing open in heaven.
And the voice I had first heard speaking to me
like a trumpet said,
"Come up here, and I will show you
what must take place after this."
*Revelation 4:1*

# Chapter Eight

## 1982

One bright day in early spring, I heard the blast of a train whistle and looked north to see a dark green locomotive headed west, hauling several dozen grain hoppers. I ran toward the train without even realizing what I was doing, overcome by some primal urge. When I was close enough, I grabbed hold of a ladder bar and swung myself up between two cars.

I thought I was somewhere near the border of Alberta. For an entire day and night I hung onto that ladder and watched the landscape roll by. The train roared past tiny, forgotten little towns and lonely farmsteads. Finally, it pulled into a siding beside twin grain elevators painted a bright orange. I jumped off before the train came to a full stop and slipped between the elevators before anyone noticed me. I saw the name NANTON blazing in white letters on the side of the building. Probably the name of the town.

Like most prairie towns I'd encountered, it was comprised of nondescript buildings of vinyl or brick, separated by weedy parking lots dotted with pickup trucks. I kept walking west, passing through a residential district and then out in the open again. Then I stopped and stared. White-capped mountains loomed on the horizon, as if bursting from the flat earth. I had spent so many years on the prairie, I'd forgotten mountains even existed.

I walked for two more days, until I made it to the foothills—

barren but for random patches of tall, skinny pine trees. Soon I entered denser woods. Good. I must be getting close to a creek—after a week without water, I was getting thirsty. I found it at the bottom of a ravine and practically dunked my whole head in, lapping water like a dog. Then I filled my canteen. The creek was bloated and fast-moving from the late winter runoff. As I contemplated crossing, the distinct sound of high-pitched, female laughter drifted through the trees.

I looked downstream to see two girls in yellow dresses balancing on a fallen log. One was dark-haired, the other blonde. The blonde attempted a pirouette and nearly fell. She shrieked—her friend giggled.

My pulse quickened, my ears roared with the chatter of the shadow people. What were they doing here, in the middle of nowhere? Remembering the incident in the diner, I quickly stowed the canteen, shouldered my guitar, and turned to climb up the bank.

Just when I was sure I'd made a clean getaway, I heard a loud splash and then a panicked scream.

"Abby! Abby! Are you all right?"

"Help! I'm stuck!"

"I can't reach you!"

I froze, took a breath. Pondered what to do. Then I dropped the guitar and the backpack and headed back into the ravine.

The dark-haired girl was on her hands and knees on the log, trying to reach her friend, who had fallen in. She was hanging onto a gnarled vine, struggling to keep her head above water. She gurgled and coughed between shrieks.

The girl on the log saw me. "Help us, please!" she screamed. "I can't reach her!"

I waded into the creek, holding steady against the forceful current. The water came up to my waist.

"It's okay," I called to the girl. "Stay still."

"My leg—stuck!"

"Just hang onto that vine—don't let go."

I ducked under the water to see that her leg was firmly caught between the two boulders. Bracing myself, I pressed my weight against one of the boulders, moving it just enough to free her foot. I resurfaced and grabbed her around the waist before the current could pull her farther downstream. She let go of the vine and went limp in my arms as I dragged her to the bank. Her head lolled, her eyes rolled as if she were about to faint. I turned her on her side and she coughed up water.

The dark-haired girl scrambled down from the log and knelt beside her friend.

"Abby! Abby! Are you okay? Talk to me, Abby!"

"Yeah. I think so. My ankle...hurts!"

"It looks sprained," I said.

The dark-haired girl looked at me with a huge smile. She was pretty, no more than fifteen. I avoided her eyes. "Thank Jehovah you came along. She could have died!" She stroked Abby's hair gently. "We are in so much trouble. What are we going to do?"

Abby moaned in reply.

"Do you live near here?" I asked.

"Not too far—we live at Promise Ranch. We were supposed to be gathering slippery elm bark, but we took a break to smoke a little weed—I guess we got carried away." She sighed. "I'm Pris, by the way. Short for Priscilla. This is Abigail. What's your name?"

"Jared."

"Jared. You're our hero."

I balked at the comment and stood up to put some distance between us. The shadow people swooned and sighed. "How far is the ranch?"

"Maybe a mile. Do you think you could carry her? I mean...I can't, and I don't think she can walk."

"Why don't you go and get help. I'll wait here with her until you get back."

"No one's going to come. Everyone's working. Please? I'm in so much trouble as it is."

I couldn't just leave them, though I desperately wanted to. Holding the girl in the water had been bad enough. Carrying her? A mile? "Well...okay, I guess. Just let me get my things."

I found my backpack and guitar and brought them back to where Pris knelt beside Abby. The injured girl seemed pretty much out of it, probably more due to marijuana than the accident. I handed Pris my belongings and bent to pick up her friend.

"You won't say anything, will you?" Abby said in a slurry voice. Her head tilted against my shoulder. Heat ran through my arm, down my side, and I found it suddenly hard to breathe.

"No, I won't."

"We aren't supposed to use it ourselves." Pris chattered as I followed her through the woods. "It's only for the customers. But everyone does it."

"You grow marijuana on your farm?"

"We grow everything ourselves. Except for trees—that's why we came into the woods."

"For the slippery—"

"Slippery Elm Bark—it makes a very good poultice for wounds and chilblains. And it can be brewed as a tea to help with stomach problems."

"You seem to know a lot about natural remedies."

"I do! It's one of my jobs. We make all our own medicine. All natural."

"You like living…out here?"

"Yes. Promise Ranch is a wonderful place. You'll see! Brother X says it is the next best place to paradise."

"Brother X?"

"He's our father—a spiritual father, you get it? The most amazing man. He's a prophet, actually."

We walked out of the woods back onto the flat plain. The outline of a working ranch appeared in the distance.

"That's it," Pris said. "Promise Ranch."

"Why is it called Promise Ranch?"

"Brother X named it after the Promised Land in the Bible. The land Jehovah promised his people."

"So this is some sort of religious commune?"

"Well, I guess so. We all live together, work together, do everything together. We're a family."

Family. The word bounced around in my head, tantalizing. The shadow people had grown strangely quiet, cooing and sighing as I carried the injured girl to her home. I should have taken that as a warning sign.

~

We came to a dirt road and a sign with PROMISE RANCH etched into its weathered wood surface. A wire fence stretched in both directions, marked with yellow flags and NO TRESPASS-ING warnings.

"What the heck happened to you two?"

A twenty-something man stood by the sign. He had long, red-dish hair and a shaggy beard, and carried a shotgun crooked over his arm. His dirty white shirt was emblazoned with the words "PROMISE SECURITY."

Pris spoke in a rush, suddenly nervous. "Oh, hey, Aaron. We were out gathering bark and Abby fell in the creek. This nice boy came along and rescued her."

The man looked me up and down with narrowed eyes. "What were *you* doing down at the creek?"

"Filling my canteen."

"You live around here?"

"Nope. Just passing through."

"No one just passes through these parts."

"He was sent from Jehovah," Pris said. "I'm sure of it. He showed up just in time!"

"Oh. Right." Aaron smirked, then took out a walkie-talkie and spoke into it: "Mimi. Code Black."

Static followed, and then a female voice crackled over the speaker. "Who is it?"

"Don't know. Pris says he rescued Abby. She's hurt."

Slight pause. Then the voice crackled again. "Send them to the house."

"Roger." Aaron stowed his walkie. "You heard her. Good luck." He grinned and tossed his head to let us pass.

We continued down the dirt road toward the ranch. Dozens of people wearing yellow shirts or dresses worked in the fields with horse-drawn plows. Ducks, goats and chickens roamed freely. More men in white shirts roamed around with shotguns. Their manner disturbed me—if this was a happy family, why did they need guns?

The compound was bigger than I first realized—barns, pad-docks, silos, and cabins surrounded the main house, a log ranch with a porch that ran the full width. Many rows of small tents lay beyond the buildings. In the front of the house stood a large white tent, the kind used for revival meetings. I'd been to some revivals in the past years, mostly traveling preachers with more salesmanship than theology.

I couldn't help but wonder what was going on at this ranch. It might have been a summer camp or a farm for wayward kids, except they were growing marijuana and had armed guards. And who was this Brother X, anyway?

The pain of holding Abby in my arms for so long became unbearable. My body shook, but I forced myself to keep walking, to breathe steadily. As we stepped onto the porch, the door opened and a tall woman came out. I assumed it was the woman called Mimi. With her dark hair caught in a bun, her white blouse and long skirt, she seemed like a throwback to the old prairie, before the modern age. In fact, the whole place felt frozen in time, which comforted me. The woman's gaze focused on the girls—she sighed and shook her head. Then she looked at me and her breath caught. Her brow furrowed slightly.

"Bring her inside," she ordered.

She directed me to set the girl on a threadbare sofa. I took a breath, relieved. The room was homey but spare, filled with cast-off furniture. A large yellow flag depicting the sun rising over a barren landscape dominated one entire wall.

"What happened this time?" The woman examined Abby's ankle as she spoke. From her exasperated tone, I assumed the girls' behavior was not a new thing.

"We were collecting bark by the creek, like you told us to, and she accidentally fell in." Pris glanced at me. "Her foot got caught—she almost drowned!"

"I can't swim," Abby said weakly, then she giggled.

Pris glared at her.

Mimi gave her a long look. "Where's the bark?"

Pris glanced down at her empty hands. "I guess I…dropped it. In all the excitement. I'll go back…"

"No, you won't. Go to your tent. I'll discuss this with Brother X."

"Please, Mimi, it won't happen again, I promise!" Pris seemed about to cry.

Mimi's expression softened. "We'll see. Now go."

Pris wiped her eyes and, with a last glance at me, disappeared out the door.

"Sarah!" Mimi called out. Another young girl came in from a different door. She wore a yellow dress with a green apron, her brown pigtails framing a pale face.

"Yes, Mimi?"

"Bring some ice and tea with turmeric, please."

"Yes, Mimi." The girl went away again.

"I'll be going then." I went to fetch the backpack and guitar Pris had left on the floor.

"The least we can do is give you some dinner for your trouble." Mimi's tone had warmed considerably. She took a step toward me. "Please stay. Brother X would want to thank you personally."

"It's not necessary."

"You must be hungry. And we can clean your clothes while you wait. You're soaking wet, and you look as though you've been traveling awhile."

"Yes, I have." Thoughts of a shower, a hot meal and a bed were hard to resist. How long had it been since I'd eaten or slept? I couldn't remember. "Well, okay."

Mimi smiled. "Come with me."

I followed her to a small log cabin behind the ranch house. A row of four neatly made cots lined one wall.

"This is the guest house. You can shower in there and rest until supper is called." She went to a closet and pulled out a black shirt and pants. "Some clothes to wear. Just leave yours by the door and we will get them washed for you."

"What does black signify?" I fingered the shirt. "I mean, I noticed that everyone seems to be—color-coded."

Mimi's mouth tightened. "Black is for the unknown. The guest. Yellow is for the Bees."

"Bees?"

"Brother X's followers. He calls them Busy Bees—they are very hard workers."

"And the white shirts?"

"The guardians. They protect the community."

"With guns?"

She bristled. "We take the safety and security of our people very seriously." She turned to the door. "I'll let you know when it's time to gather for the meal. I'm sure you have many questions, which I cannot answer until and unless you choose to become one of us."

"One of you?"

"You seem as though you need a place to belong. The harvest is plentiful, but the workers are few." She smiled slightly and left.

*A place to belong.* Could this be such a place? I'd always been separate, set apart, different. Unable to assimilate. Perhaps my happening upon those two girls at the creek had been a kind of destiny, leading me here, to Promise Ranch.

I shed my filthy clothes, took a shower and put on the new pants and shirt. It felt good to be clean. I put my old clothes by the door, but when I tried to open it, I found it was locked. From the outside.

I frowned. Why did Mimi lock me in? Perhaps these people were wary of strangers.

I lay down on one of the cots. A few minutes later there was a soft knock at the door.

"Come in."

The lock clicked and the door opened. The girl named Sarah appeared, a steaming mug in her hand.

"Mimi thought you might like some tea." Her voice trembled, like she was scared. She had no idea I was more afraid of her than she was of me.

"Uh...sure." I got up to take the mug from her.

"I made it myself. It's chamomile. And...other things."

"Oh. Thank you."

She stood a moment longer, staring at me. I turned away, feeling an inner heat rise at her perusal.

"Sorry!" She gathered up my dirty clothes and fled from the room. The lock clicked again.

I took a sip—the tea was earthy and slightly bitter with a sharp aroma, like skunk. Not like any chamomile I'd ever tasted. But it warmed my throat and made me feel suddenly more relaxed. I finished the tea and lay down on the cot, replaying the events of the last hours over and over again. Was I truly meant to be here? Could I have finally found, at long last, my home?

# Chapter Nine

"Supper is ready."

I bolted upright and blinked, forgetting for a moment where I was. Mimi stood framed in the doorway, Aaron at her side. I was surprised to discover I'd actually fallen asleep.

"You must be hungry. Come along."

I scrambled from the cot and followed them out to the big tent. People sat eating at long trestle tables with the food tables at one end. There had to be over two hundred diners, almost all wearing yellow. Women, men, teenagers and children sat apart from each other, chatting happily. Teen girls at one table stopped eating to stare at me and giggle. I didn't see Pris or Abby. A few of the white-shirts were scattered among them, while others patrolled the perimeter. The food workers wore green aprons. Sarah was one of them.

Mimi handed me a plate and told me to get in line. The servers deposited scoopfuls of steamed vegetables and rice onto my plate. At the end of the row was a basket of rolls and pitchers of water and milk. Also a large dispenser of a murky green-brown liquid I assumed to be tea. Meager fare for such a large group of people.

"We grow all our food ourselves," said Mimi, as if in answer to my unasked question. "We eat whatever Jehovah provides."

She led me to a group of men seated together. I had a sudden flashback to my first day at Saint James School, a tableful of boys staring at me with hostile intent.

"This is Jared." Mimi said. "He is a visitor. Please be welcoming, as we owe him a debt of gratitude. We are hoping he will stay with us."

Unlike the Saint James boys, these men nodded and made room for me. I took in their wiry builds and sallow expressions, their unshaven faces and the dirt under their fingernails. Their yellow shirts were sweat-stained, and they smelled powerfully of manure and sawdust.

"Thanks," I said.

"Name's Abel." The man opposite me looked to be around thirty, though he was missing several teeth. He introduced me to the others. "This is Isaac, Jacob, Nathan and Zack." They mumbled greetings. "Welcome to Promise Ranch. Where you from?"

"Niagara."

"Niagara? You're a long way from home. Did you run away?"

"I guess so."

"What were you running from?"

*Myself.* "Just needed to be on my own."

"I did the same thing." Abel chuckled. "Dropped out of college, rattled around Vancouver, smoked a lot of dope. Needed something real, eh? I mean, life, man—what was it? College, job, marriage, two point four kids—what's the point, eh? Then one day, I went to this coffee shop and there was Brother X playing his guitar with this band he had back then. The songs he sang—so real, man! Truth! He was singing what I was feeling, get what I'm saying? I went up to talk to him after—we talked all night, man. Went back every day. When he came out to the ranch here—I came too. Never looked back."

"Why does he call himself Brother X?" I asked.

"We're all brothers." Isaac, a forty-something with long blond hair and a beard, spoke up. "Brothers in the Universe. We are all one. Names don't matter."

"How did you find us?" Zack, the oldest among them, pushed away his plate and set his elbows on the table. A subtle edge to his tone made me feel I was under interrogation.

"I was just walking—west. Hopped a train, ended up here."

"I used to do that," said Isaac. "Hop trains. Just driftin'. This is a good place to land. I mean, it's hard work and all, but we're building something here. Something important."

"What, exactly?"

"Kind of like—the Ark." The others nodded, though I had no idea what that meant.

"You ought to stay," said Abel. "We always need more Bees. Besides, you don't want to be out there when it happens."

"When what happens?"

A bell rang and, without hesitation, everyone picked up their plates and shuffled toward the food tables, now loaded with dish pans. I followed along, still thinking about Abel's warning. What were they expecting to happen?

A female worker stared at the uneaten food on my plate. She glanced at me, then to my surprise she pulled open the pocket of her green apron and tipped the plate into it.

"Waste not, want not," she said with a bright smile.

I turned away to find Mimi and Aaron waiting for me.

"Did you enjoy your meal?"

"Sure," I said. "Thanks. How are Abby and Pris? I didn't see them—"

"They're fine. I thought perhaps you'd like a tour."

"Sure, okay."

For an hour we toured the compound, Aaron trailing behind us. Everyone was back at work, even the field hands. Mimi talked as we walked. "As I said before, we make everything ourselves. We pride ourselves on our self-sufficiency. But it's a lot of work. Some of our people only get three hours sleep a night." She showed me barns, the greenhouses, the kitchens, the food processing centers, baking ovens, and the sewing and yarn-making facilities. Children worked right alongside adults. No one was idle. The workers looked up and smiled as we passed, offering greetings of welcome. Mimi often paused to share a word of praise or bent to pat the head of a child. She knew everyone's name.

We passed by the rows of tents, which Mimi referred to as the "hive."

"Most of the workers live here. It's a temporary measure, until we get more dorms built."

"What's that place?" I pointed to a plain, white steel building that seemed set apart from the rest.

"That's the…lab," Mimi said. "Where we make the herbal

remedies we sell to health food stores. It's an important source of income." She did not take me into that building. Instead, we headed back to the guest house. Darkness had fallen by then. "We don't show off our community to just anyone, you know. Brother X believes you are deserving. Because of how you rescued Abigail."

"So you told him about that?"

"I tell him everything. You will meet him tomorrow at the sunrise service. I hope you don't mind getting up early."

"I always do."

"You have some ranch experience, I presume?"

"Yes. Plenty."

"Then you will fit right in." We stopped before the door of the guest house. "I'll pick you up at 5:30 AM."

"I was wondering—Abel said something about building an Ark—?"

"Just a figure of speech."

"Are you expecting a flood?"

"Out here?" She smiled. "Not that sort of flood."

"How long have you been here?"

"About five years now. We started the ministry in Vancouver over twenty years ago. Back then it was Brother X and me." She paused, looking wistful. "He took me in when I was young and alone. He taught me about Jehovah, about his great and mighty works in the Flood, the Exodus. And the time to come. He was the most amazing man I'd ever known." Her gaze faded, as if she were lost in the past. Then she blinked and shook her head. "Sleep well, Brother Jared."

*Brother.*

# Chapter Ten

The revival tent was filled to capacity the next morning, people either standing or kneeling, as the chairs had been removed and the tables grouped together to form a stage. Torches flickered in the pre-dawn dark, along with the maniacally prancing shadow people. They seemed delighted with this place. But why? The shadow people hated Jehovah, hated anything to do with God.

I couldn't help but think of my old days in the circus—the atmosphere felt strangely similar. A group of musicians on the stage played songs I'd never heard in a church—folk songs by Bob Dylan and John Denver with the words changed to make them sound more spiritual. What they lacked in polish they made up for in enthusiasm—they had the whole tent clapping, singing and dancing. All except for the white-shirts, who stood at the side, watching with blank faces.

As dawn broke, the band stopped playing and the lead singer shouted, "Prepare the way!" The crowd fell to a hush and dropped to their knees. I glanced around to see a long black limo pull up alongside the tent. A door opened and a man stepped out. My first glimpse of Brother X.

He was remarkably tall, dressed in a long white robe tied with a red sash. With his narrow, imperious face, bald head, and long beard, he could have been forty or eighty. Though his skin was smooth and unwrinkled, he had the air of an ancient deity. A group of young girls in yellow dresses ran over to throw rose petals on the ground before him as he walked up to the stage. The crowd chanted, "Prepare the way! Prepare the way!"

Brother X ascended to the platform just as slanting rays of sun poured into the tent, illuminating his face. He sat on an ornate upholstered chair that hadn't been there a moment ago and folded his hands together in prayer. The chanting stopped.

"My children, my friends, Jehovah loves you. And I love you."

His voice was soft and musical, slightly accented, probably French-Canadian. The congregation responded as one voice: "We love you, Brother."

"Know that I love you, and I will always love you, no matter the width or breadth of your disobedience. I love as Jehovah loves. And you, my children, must love me in the same way. Without reservation. With joy in your heart. For this is the essence of life. To love and be loved. To give yourself wholly and completely over to love in all its forms, for Jehovah created all love for his glory."

He continued in this vein for a while, speaking of love and Jehovah. But then his tone changed, became more forceful and urgent, as he spoke of the coming end times. He stood up, paced back and forth, gesticulated dramatically. His voice trembled as he spoke of the terrible destruction that would burst forth at the world's judgment, and how they—his people—were the only ones who would escape.

"Jehovah promised after the Flood that he would never again destroy the world by water. No, the next time, it would be by fire! And this will happen soon—very soon! The arms race is escalating, the world is headed toward nuclear winter. We alone will survive, because we are prepared. Jehovah will protect us! It is we who will live to see the renewing of the world!"

The congregation cheered hysterically. The band played a rousing rock song and everyone joined in, singing, "*Waiting for the end of the world, waiting for the end of the world, dear Lord, I sincerely hope you're coming 'cause you really started something…*"

The music ground in my ears as Brother X stepped down from the platform and waded into the crowd of adorers. His followers screamed and jumped and reached out to touch him, to grab hold of his robe. They wailed and sobbed and sang out with a kind of wild joy I'd never witnessed before, not even in the most spirited revival meeting.

I was mesmerized. The shadow people wrapped their tendrils around my limbs, drawing me toward this man, entangling my spirit with his. I heard a voice that sounded like my mother's:

*Resist. Resist Resist.*

I didn't want to resist. I wanted to *bask*. The pleasure of this new sensation overwhelmed me. I rose, and the music and passion seemed to rise with me as I approached Brother X. He turned suddenly, as if aware of my presence.

"Brother Jared. Welcome." His words washed over me like cool water. He took my face in his hands and kissed my cheek. Then he wrapped his arms around me. And I was truly lost.

# Chapter Eleven

"Does that happen often?"

I gazed at Brother X, sprawled on a purple velvet sofa, strumming a guitar. *My* guitar, I realized. His white robe hung open to reveal a Grateful Dead T-shirt and torn denim shorts. His fingers moved lazily over the fretboard, playing a soft rift over and over.

I took in my surroundings—an array of stuffed furniture, shag rugs, hanging beads, and huge, soft pillows. A far cry from the austere ranch house. Where was I, exactly? How did I get here? The last thing I remembered was Brother X embracing me. My body felt light and tingly, flooded in warmth. I raised my hand to look at it—whiter than usual, almost luminous.

"Does what happen?" I asked.

"The glow."

"Glow?"

"Yeah, man. You glowed, like Moses returning from the mountain. It was far out." He spoke languidly, with none of the spell-binding cadence of his preaching. He started to sing.

*Don't look back*
*Love is here*
*Don't look back*
*The end is near*
*Our time has come*
*We'll be as one*

*Forever and always*
*Love has won*

He grinned. "What you think, man? You like my song? Just wrote that. I used to have a band. Back in Vancouver. The Doomsday Prophets. We put out an album. Had a lot of gigs, lots of groupies. We could have been great. But Jehovah had other plans for me." He set the guitar aside. "Did you enjoy the service this morning?"

"I…I…well, it was a lot different from any church I've been to before."

He laughed, a deep, throaty sound. "That's a good thing, right?"

"Yes. And the sermon—what was that about—nuclear winter?"

"It's coming, man. The nations strive to destroy each other. Jehovah said to me: Prepare! Take your hive into the desert!" He shrugged. "So that is what I did. The problem is, we've been here a long time. Waiting. The Bees are getting restless. They keep asking me, when will it happen? How long must we wait? So I prayed to Jehovah for a sign. And then…you came."

"It was only by chance that I was passing through—"

"Nothing is by chance!" He leaned toward me. "Tell me, Brother Jared, haven't you thought all your life that there is something different about you? That you are not like other people?"

I swallowed. Nodded.

"Same for me. Ever since I was a little boy, I knew I was different. Set apart for something…greater. That is how I recognized you, from the moment you set foot on Promise Ranch—"

"You *recognized* me?"

"**Because I** was expecting you! The answer to my prayer! You are meant to be here. You were *sent*."

I stared at him but said nothing.

"I must meditate for a time, to hear what Jehovah has to say about this. You will wait until I am ready to declare the mission for the coming age."

"I'm sorry, but I can't," I said. "I have to be on my way."

His eyes seemed to vibrate. "Oh man, don't do that. You know you don't want to leave." His voice…soft and yet hard, like velvet over steel. I nodded.

He clapped his hands, making me jump.

"David! Where's my tea?"

A yellow-shirted teenage boy with glazed eyes appeared. He set the tray he carried on a table and, with a wan smile, handed me one of the two teacups it held. I took the cup and thanked him. The boy presented the other cup to Brother X with a deep bow.

"Thank you, my child. You may go." Brother X patted the boy's head as he took the cup. The boy scurried out.

"To Brother Jared!" Brother X made a toast and downed his tea in a single gulp. I took a sip—as before, the warmth sped through my veins, loosening my muscles, fogging my brain.

My host settled back and strummed my guitar idly, eyes closed. I got up and wandered around. Vases, sculptures, books, and religious icons filled every table and bookshelf . Statues of the Virgin Mary sat next to solid-gold Buddhas. A huge tapestry of a weeping Jesus, crowned in thorns, adorned one wall. Prayer beads lay on tables and hung on objects. Pots of incense filled the room with sharp, tingly aromas.

After a long time, Brother X finally spoke again. "Yes!"

I spun around to see him with one hand in the air, face tilted up, as if he were speaking to the ceiling. Then he fished a walkie-talkie out of the cushion of the sofa. "Mimi! Come!"

Mimi appeared within seconds, looking flustered.

"Mimi! Jehovah has told me who this man is! He is the Messenger!"

Mimi paled. "The Messenger?"

"Yes, yes! The angel sent by God—like the one who appeared to Joshua before the walls of Jericho fell!"

Mimi glanced at me. "An...angel?"

"You saw how he lit up this morning—only an angel could do that! Yes, he has come to proclaim God's judgment! The war is imminent! We must prepare! Call the Bees—we must begin tonight!"

"But Jere—Brother X, the Bees have to work. Can't this wait until tomorrow?"

"My love." Brother X went to her, stroked her cheek. "Will the end of the world wait until we are ready? No. Every soul must prepare. Come now." He drew her into a warm embrace, held her for several seconds. She seemed to melt in his arms. He kissed her so passionately I had to turn away. "There now, better? Go, prepare the way. Tonight."

"Yes..." she murmured as he released her. "Of course, Brother."

"I love you."

"I love you."

Mimi turned in a kind of trance and left. As soon as she was gone, Brother X whirled around and clapped his hands.

"Jared, Jared! What a day this will be! What a glorious day! Jehovah be praised!" He grabbed my arms and spun me around in his mad dance, singing the end of the world song the band had played that morning. I couldn't help but dance with him.

# Chapter Twelve

That night, dressed in a white silk robe and gold sash to match Brother X, I got into the black limo which was surrounded by a platoon of white-shirts. The day had been a waking dream of which I couldn't account for several hours. I had bathed in a tub the size of a small swimming pool and drank a great deal of the bitter tea. I don't remember dressing myself. From the backseat of the limo, I stared up at the dwelling I'd just left. Far grander than I had realized, the house was an actual mansion.

"How are you feeling, Messenger?" Brother X draped his arm around my shoulders.

"A little—weird."

"Good! Weird is good. We are going to have some fun tonight!"

A caravan of black cars preceded the limo through a tall iron gate and down a winding, narrow mountain road shrouded in trees. It must have been more than three miles long. At the entrance of the ranch, people lined the road, holding candles and chanting. When we pulled up to the big tent, white-shirts jumped out to push back the people swarming the car. Excitement crackled in the air, people already stirred into a frenzy. Music throbbed from inside the tent, accompanied by exuberant singing.

Aaron grabbed my arm as I stepped out and hustled me toward the back of the stage, concealed behind a curtain. He put his finger to his lips and indicated I should wait. Then I heard Brother X's melodious voice addressing his people:

"My children! Many of you have wondered when our prayers for deliverance would be answered. I told you to watch and wait. Jehovah is never late, though he may seem to tarry. I called this special meeting to tell you something great: Your prayers have been heard!"

The crowd cheered.

"We have been visited, dear children, by an actual angel of Jehovah! Yes! He came in the guise of an ordinary man, just as angels always appeared in the scriptures. We thought he was an Unknown! But he *was* known, oh, how he was known. As soon as I laid eyes on him, I was able to see him for who he really was. My children, I give you, Jehovah's own Messenger!"

Thunderous cheers and chants. Aaron pushed me out through a crack in the curtain. I stood stock still before an ecstatic crowd, unable to see very much in the dim torchlight. Then something heavy descended upon my shoulders and Brother X whispered in my ear: "Spread out your arms." I did as I was told. The crowd suddenly quieted.

Then a voice boomed over a loudspeaker, no longer Brother X's voice but a deep, resonant voice like the voice of God:

"Jehovah has spoken! Jehovah has spoken! The day you've been waiting for is at hand! Now is the time for the cleansing to begin!"

The crowd responded with loud wails and cries, shrieks of terror. The sound was like a bolt of electricity shooting through my body, breaking me open. My very being seemed to dissolve in an inferno of light that filled the tent, turned the night to day. The light came from—me. Brutal heat scorched my skin, igniting every nerve and sinew—I could almost feel my blood begin to boil. The crowd reacted with gasps and swoons, bowing down before me. I twisted my head to see what had been set upon my shoulders. I should have known.

A gigantic pair of wings.

# Chapter Thirteen

We were back in the car, headed up the mountain. I felt dazed, my head fuzzy, my body still prickling with heat. I opened the window to let the cold night air blast my face. My throat burned with a powerful thirst.

"That was beautiful." An over-excited Brother X giggled. "You should have seen yourself! Oh, how magnificent you were! It was a true miracle of Jehovah."

"How did you do it?"

"What? The wings?"

"No. Not the wings. The…glow."

"The glow? Ha! I didn't do that. That was all you, my friend. I told you before."

I shook my head. "No. No, that's not me…"

"Oh, Jared, Jared." He wrapped one arm around my shoulders and pulled me to him. "You have no idea how special you are, do you? You have spent your whole life unaware of your own gifts. Jehovah created you to be what you are. Why can't you accept who you are and love yourself for it?"

"Love myself?"

"All love begins with self-love. We can't love others if we hate ourselves. You've hated yourself all your life. You've thought you were some kind of mistake. Isn't that right?"

I nodded.

"I knew it! Your coming here is proof that you are far from a mistake. You are anointed! As I am. As were Elijah and Moses and Noah and Joseph and David. They thought they were worthless until Jehovah showed them their true path, their true purpose!"

Could this be true? All these years I had thought of myself as an abomination. A hideous mistake. Maybe Brother X was right, maybe I did have a purpose. Jehovah's purpose. And it took this strange yet magnetic man to make me see it.

"You will be at my side from now on," Brother X went on. "My guardian angel. My protector. And our judge."

I looked at him. "Judge?"

"Yes! There is evil lurking in our midst, Jared. Not every Bee is a child of Jehovah. I know it. It happened even to Moses—his own brother and sister conspired against him! They were punished by Jehovah. So too, we must root out those whose hearts are not fully committed. That is what the Cleansing is for."

"What happens in the Cleansing?"

He laughed. "You'll see!"

We arrived at the mansion. Mimi was already there. Brother X greeted her with another affectionate hug and kiss. I wondered about their relationship—Mimi was clearly in love with the man.

"We will begin at dawn. Sleep well, Messenger!" Brother X sang out as he enfolded me in his arms. I felt again the tangling of his spirit with mine, as if I were being cocooned. Hugging seemed to be his thing.

He disappeared through the door. Mimi smiled at me.

"This way, Messenger."

She took me to a bedroom on the third floor filled with more stuffed furniture and a large, canopied bed covered with a red velvet bedspread. A tray of hot tea sat on an antique table, along with a plate of fruit and cheese. Heavy red curtains hung on the windows.

"If you need anything, just ask Aaron. He will be right outside."

"All night?"

"Yes."

"Could I have my…guitar?"

She hesitated. "I will ask Brother X." She retreated.

Aaron peered in. "Good night, Messenger."

"Wait. Can I ask you something?"

He hesitated, the door half-closed. "Of course, Messenger."

"How did you...come to be here?"

He shrugged. "I've always been here, I suppose."

"So you have parents here then?"

"Parents? No."

"What about a wife? Children?"

"No, no. We are not allowed to have wives."

"Not allowed?"

"Not in this world. But in the next world, we can have as many wives as we want."

"If you aren't allowed, then where did all the children come from?"

"The children?" He looked at me, perplexed. "All are children of Brother X."

I nodded slowly. "Thanks for explaining that."

"No problem."

He shut the door. The lock clicked. I lay on the bed and stared into the canopy, trying to sort all of this out. I knew so little about mothers and fathers, husbands and wives. But I had never heard of one man being the father of so many children. Except perhaps for Jacob in the Bible—he had had many children. Perhaps Brother X was like Jacob.

I drank the tea, letting it rush through my body and relax my mind. Maybe I would be able to sleep again. No sooner had I started to drift off when the sound of a car motor outside brought me back to my senses. I went to the window, pulled aside the curtain, and frowned. The window was barred.

I looked down into the main courtyard where a shiny black car idled before the entrance. The back door opened, and a woman got out. Not a woman though...a girl. In a yellow dress. She hesitated, staring up at the mansion in wonder. A light from the doorway caught her face. Pris. A white-shirt nudged her inside.

I went to the door—locked. Unsettled, I returned to the window and watched the car. It remained in the drive for over an hour with white-shirts standing guard. Then there was some commotion and Pris re-appeared. She seemed to have trouble walking—she was bent over, her hair disheveled. She looked as though she were…crying. A white-shirt put her back in the car.

What had happened to her? Had Brother X punished her for what happened at the creek?

The car pulled away and drove slowly out of the gate. Several white-shirts remained in the courtyard. My stomach clenched with something I had never fully experienced before—anger.

I went to the other window and pulled aside the curtain. Bars. This window looked down on a walled garden. No white-shirts there. I grabbed hold of the iron bars and pulled. Heat surged through me, seeming to melt the iron to my will. When the hole was big enough, I squeezed through, jumped to the ground, took a running leap and cleared the ten-foot wall easily. My heart thudding, I ran through the woods until I saw the taillights of the car headed down the mountain. I followed, keeping my distance.

The car drove straight to the tent area of the ranch. I hid behind the outhouses as Pris got out and stumbled down a row of tents, accompanied by a white-shirt. I decided to wait until the white-shirt returned to the car, then I would go and see if she was okay.

The white-shirt re-appeared a few minutes later, but he wasn't alone. He led another girl by the hand—this one even younger than Pris. The girl carried a doll in her free hand. She looked scared. The white-shirt picked her up and put her in the car.

Something was wrong. Why were little girls being taken to the mansion in the middle of the night? The unfamiliar anger swelled inside me—heat prickled my skin. Instead of finding Pris, I raced ahead of the car up the mountain road.

I stopped in the woods and looked around for some idea— my gaze fell upon a thick, half-dead tree leaning at a precarious angle. I gave it a few hard shoves until it made a great crackling sound and crashed onto the road. I hid in the brush and waited. A few seconds later, the headlights of the black car came into view. It stopped abruptly and the two white-shirts got out. They scratched their heads and swore.

"That thing wasn't there a minute ago. How did this happen?"

They tried to manhandle the tree out of the way.

"We could walk up," said one of them.

"It's two miles! Can you radio the house? Tell them we need a crew to move the tree."

One of the white-shirts opened the driver door to retrieve the walkie-talkie. I jumped out onto the top of the tree, summoning all the rage within me I had held so long in check. I felt my body burn like a torch in the night.

"What the heck—?" The white-shirt at the car dropped the walkie-talkie. The other one staggered backward, covering his eyes.

"Take that child back to her tent!" I shouted as loud as I could, my voice strange and fiery in my own ears.

"It's...the angel!" one of them exclaimed.

"Take her back!" I shouted.

My body blazed so hot I thought I might set fire to the trees. I breathed through the heat, absorbing it as a part of my essential being. *This* was what I was made of. Just as Brother X said.

The two men scrambled back into the car, started the engine and threw the transmission into reverse. They would have to back all the way down the road, which would take some time. The walkie-talkie lay on the ground. That was fortunate.

Once they were out of sight, I hiked up to Brother X's mansion. I climbed over the wall into the garden, scrambled up the side of the house to my room, bent the bars back into place and got into bed.

Several minutes later, Brother X threw open my door, Aaron at his side. I sat up in bed and rubbed my eyes as if I'd been fast sleep. I hoped neither of them could hear my pounding heart.

"What did you do?" Brother X's tone was savage, the honey turned to vinegar.

"What are you talking about?"

He moved toward me, his blue eyes almost black with rage and fear. "My men saw you on the road."

"Wasn't me," I said. "I was asleep."

"He never left the room," Aaron said hurriedly. "I was here! I would have seen—"

Brother X's gaze went to the window—I'd left the curtain open. He lurched over and ran his hands up and down the bars. Were they perfectly straight or still slightly bent? I hadn't had time to make sure.

After a moment, he turned from the window and came to me. He bent over me and touched my face—he pulled his hand away as if he'd been burned.

"Why are you so—hot?"

"I don't know," I said. "I was having...a bad dream. There were all these children crying and bombs going off everywhere. Perhaps Jehovah was giving me another message."

His head tilted, eyes narrowed. He was about to say something else but then glanced at Aaron and shut his mouth.

"Well, then, you should go back to sleep, to get the rest of the message. It could be important."

"Yes, it must be very important."

He straightened, glanced at Aaron, then strode out of the room. Aaron followed, shutting the door. The lock clicked.

I lay back in the bed and smiled. Maybe being an angel wasn't such a bad gig after all.

# Chapter Fourteen

I should have left then. Gone out the window and disappeared.

But I didn't.

In the weeks, months and years that followed, I would ask myself why. Perhaps it was hubris—I had Brother X over a barrel. He'd created me. He couldn't destroy me. And I was the only one on this ranch who could stop him. For once in my life, I could do something good.

I sat in the chair and waited for morning. Before the sun rose, the lock clicked and the door opened. Mimi stood in the portal. Her hair fell unbound over her shoulders, and her lips looked redder, as if she'd put on lipstick. She'd changed her clothes as well, exchanging her skirt for a white robe similar to Brother X's and mine.

"Did you sleep well?" she asked pleasantly.

"Great," I lied.

"Well, then, we should be going."

"Where is Brother X?"

"He has already left. Wanted to prepare the Bees for your...arrival." She spoke in a clipped tone and didn't make eye contact. A wave of apprehension slid through me. I followed her into the hall. Aaron was there, along with a couple more white-shirts. They watched me in silence as I passed by.

*Run.*

*No.*

I got into the waiting car. Aaron sat beside me, his gun across his knees. Mimi sat in the front seat. I couldn't see the driver, another white-shirt.

"So, what happens during these cleansing ceremonies?" I asked Mimi.

"We've never had one before."

"Never?"

"We were waiting." She glanced back at me. "For you."

White-shirts surrounded the car when we arrived at the big tent. Several of them flanked me and led me inside.

No music this time, just a low hum, barely audible. The whole tent seemed to be consumed in a dense fog, making it difficult to see much of the surroundings. My eyes burned.

The white-shirts led me down the torch-lined center aisle. People were on their knees on either side, their faces to the ground. They were chanting: "Jehovah, forgive us." Brother X stood on the stage. He appeared to be praying, his eyes closed, mouthing words that didn't make sense to me. Behind him stood a large wooden cross.

The white-shirts pushed me up onto the stage. Brother X turned to me, and with a ghostly smile put his hands on my shoulders. He kissed me on both cheeks.

"My children!" His voice rang out. The people stopped chanting and raised their heads. "Today is a great day. The day we have been waiting for! Today, you will be cleansed of your sins and all the evil that you hold in your hearts. I prayed all night for your deliverance. And here is what Jehovah has revealed to me. This man!" He pointed to me. "This man, whom I believed was an angel sent by Jehovah to judge you, is not an angel at all!"

The crowd gasped.

"It's true. I was wrong. Dead wrong. He is not the Messenger. Jehovah has set me straight on that point. He is not here to judge you. He is here to take your sins upon himself. To die in your place! This man is the returned Christ!"

I stared at him, stunned. The audience seemed equally stunned—they swooned in collective ecstasy, shouting words of praise.

Brother X cried out. "Jehovah forgives! Jehovah forgives!"

The audience picked up the chant. "Jehovah forgives!"

Before I even knew what was happening, four white-shirts hauled me to the cross, holding my arms out. Brother X stood before me, a hammer and nail in his hands. He leered at me, his eyes blazing with malice.

"Jehovah has spoken. Prepare to take away our sins."

He pressed the nail into my open palm. My mind raced, my body exploded with heat. I felt the nail drive through my hand into the cross—what pain there was only enraged me. I swung my other hand and drove my fist into Brother X's jaw. He sprawled across the stage as people gasped and screamed. More white-shirts piled on me—I felt the nail drive into my other hand. My body became light and heat that poured out over the screaming crowd. Brother X's voice rose up, echoed a million times:

"Jehovah forgives you!"

"Jehovah forgives us!"

The shadow people took over, wrapping me in their sinewy tendrils, laughing with glee. I heard the Voice, breaking through the haze of light and noise, speaking words of love.

*You are my son.*

And then the Voice told me his name.

I sighed and let my head drop to my chest. *Submit. Submit.* It was over now. This was the proper end of my story. The shadow people sang their songs of death.

But then another sound invaded my deadened mind. A high-pitched, undulating whine.

A siren.

# Chapter Fifteen

"Everyone on the ground! Now!"

Something new was happening, but I couldn't quite figure it out. Flashing lights of blue and red intermingled with the torchlight. Screaming, no longer in worship but in sheer panic. A voice on a bullhorn. The explosion of a gunshot. More screams, people running, trampling over each other.

I wrenched my hands from the cross and pulled the nails out of my bleeding palms. I felt no pain. Just…numbness. Brother X was nowhere to be seen, nor were any of the white-shirts. Several people lay on the ground with hands over their heads.

The voice on the bullhorn blasted: "Drop your weapon!"

Peering through the lights and the fog, I spotted Aaron crouched behind a stack of speakers. He cocked the weapon and fired again. A girl running past him collapsed, blood spreading on her yellow dress. Pris? No…Sarah.

Aaron paused to reload as the police continued to shout at him. I calculated the distance—about twenty feet. Drawing a deep breath, I jumped from the stage, sailed through the air and landed on top of him, knocking the gun from his hands. He turned on me with rage-filled eyes, but I held him down until the Mounties surrounded us. I let go as they pulled me from Aaron's body, thrust me face down on the ground and shackled my hands behind my back. Through the shuffling of black boots, I watched the light drain from Sarah's eyes.

⁓

For three hours I sat in a small cinderblock room, my hands, cleaned of blood, cuffed to the metal table. Once, a female sergeant brought me a glass of water. I asked where Brother X was. She said she didn't know. I asked about Sarah. She shook her head.

Finally, the door opened and a Mountie entered, followed by a man in a rumpled suit with a pronounced comb-over. He sat heavily opposite me and tossed a file on the table.

"Sorry to keep you waiting." He had an English accent. "I'm Detective Constable Wainwright of the RCMP in Calgary." He opened the file. "Let's start with your name."

"Jared. Laurent."

"Okay, Jared. What was your affiliation with Jeremiah Langston?"

"Who?"

"Brother X."

"I only met him yesterday."

"Really?" He cocked an eyebrow. "How did that happen?"

"I was passing through—there was a girl drowning and I helped her—took her to the ranch. They wouldn't let me leave."

"They imprisoned you?"

"They locked me in a room."

"Hmmm." Wainwright consulted his notes. "What happened this morning?"

"Brother X tried to kill me. He nailed me to a cross."

Wainwright shifted in his seat. "May I see your hands?"

I opened my palms. The detective examined them with furrowed brow.

"I don't see any wounds."

Of course not. The wounds had already healed. I closed my fists. Wainwright consulted his file. "We've been watching Brother X and his flock, or should I say *hive*, for several months. Loonies in the boonies have always been a problem in these parts. And then we got an anonymous tip about a marijuana operation from someone on the ranch. That's why we were able to stage the raid this morning."

"I don't know anything about the drugs. All I know is that Brother X has total control over the people on that ranch. And he uses his power to do things—"

"Well, not so fast. Langston claims that *you* are the leader, not him."

"Me?" My jaw dropped open. "I only got to the ranch day before yesterday."

"He says different. He says he was just a mouthpiece for you. The others say the same thing. You claimed to be Jesus Christ, and you staged the whole crucifixion scene yourself. Got the idea from that Manson fellow in California a few years back."

"That's a lie."

"Langston has a broken jaw. And you look...unhurt."

I inhaled slowly, trying to organize my thoughts. "They're lying. Ask Abby—the girl I rescued. Ask Pris."

Wainwright wrote down the names. "We've talked to all the girls. They all say the same thing. You were the leader."

"What about Mimi? Have you talked to her?"

"Who?"

"Mimi. She ran the place. A woman, forty-something, dark hair. Didn't you arrest her too?"

"I haven't seen anyone matching that description."

"If you've been keeping tabs on Brother X, you must know about her."

"We didn't know about *you*."

I sighed. "I'm telling you the truth. Brother X tried to kill me."

"Why?"

"Because I tried to stop him from hurting a girl at the ranch."

"Hurting?"

I told him about seeing Pris and the other little girl. My suspicions. He listened in silence. "Did you see Brother X actually...abusing the girl?"

"I didn't see it. But I saw what she looked like after."

"We've talked to many of the girls. None of them have reported any sort of...abuse. As far as the crucifixion thing, Brother X says he was only following orders. *Your* orders."

"How can you believe anything he says?"

"How can I believe *you*?"

"I stopped the shooter," I said. "The one who shot Sarah—Aaron. Why would I do that if I was responsible for all this? Why wouldn't I just run if I had the chance?"

That gave him pause. He looked at the Mountie standing by the door. "That true?"

"I don't know, sir. I didn't see it."

"Well, find out who did."

"Yes, sir." The Mountie left the room.

I tried again. "Detective Constable, you can call my family in Niagara. They'll tell you—"

"Already did."

The detective knew more about me than he had let on. "Then you know I've never been to Vancouver—"

"I talked to a woman—Monique? Stepmother, maybe? She claims they haven't seen you in ten years. They don't know where you've been. When I told her about the charges leveled against you, she said she absolutely believed that you were capable of this. She practically called you a sociopath."

I closed my eyes. *Monique. Of course she did.*

"Detective Constable," I said slowly, "don't you think I'm a little too young to have been giving Brother X his marching orders for the past ten years?"

"We haven't been tracking him for ten years. Only the last eighteen months. And that's only because the neighboring ranchers complained."

"About what?"

"Promise Ranch wouldn't allow them to move cattle through their land to the summer pastures, a courtesy that's always been extended amongst ranchers. They'd posted armed guards and shot at anyone who tried. That's not very neighborly conduct. We've had weapons and drug allegations but didn't get anything concrete until the raid this morning. Now we have a dead girl in addition to a compound full of illegal drugs. We are going to have to charge you with drug trafficking and conspiracy to murder."

"But I didn't do it!"

"You'll have a chance to prove your innocence. Do you want to call a lawyer?"

"Yes."

They provided me a phone.
I called Ralph.

# Chapter Sixteen

He was around twenty-seven, I figured. It'd been ten years since I last saw him, and that hadn't ended on good terms. He might have moved, or changed his number. He might have forgotten all about me.

The only number I had was the one in Niagara. I dialed it, and prayed that Monique didn't answer. *One. Two. Three. Four.* My heart sank. Then there was a click, and a female voice answered, heavily accented. I let out a breath.

"Laurent residence."

"Hello, Rhianne. This is…Jared."

She gasped. "Jared? Mon dieu! Jared! We thought you dead!"

"Please, don't tell Rafe I called," I said. "Can you let me talk to Ralph?"

"Ralph, no more here! He live in Hamilton!"

"Can you give me the number?"

"Oh…I don't know…"

"Please, Rhianne. It's a matter of life and death."

"Okay, one moment." She must have set down the receiver. I heard some commotion in the background and feared she was telling Rafe or Monique I was on the line. I was prepared to hang up, but then I heard her voice again, speaking very softly.

"Here's the number."

"Thank you. And please don't tell anyone I called, okay?

Promise?"

"Yes, okay. I promise, Monsieur Jared."

"Thank you."

I hung up and dialed Ralph's number.

"Ralph speaking," said a mature voice in a clipped tone.

I swallowed the lump in my throat. "Hi, Ralph. It's…Jared."

Long pause.

"Jared?" His voice rose—skeptical.

"Yes. It's me."

"Where are you?"

"I'm… out west. Alberta."

"Alberta! Good Lord. I thought you were dead."

"Worse. I'm in jail."

~

"You made bail, kid," said the guard, unlocking my cell. "Your brother came for you. He brought you some clothes."

I was taken to a small room with no windows. A paper bag sat on a table. I opened it and pulled out jeans and a plaid shirt. I smiled. They were my old clothes from home. I changed and knocked on the door. Half an hour later, I was released to the outside.

I blinked in the bright sunlight—it had been almost two weeks since I saw the sun. When my eyes adjusted, I spotted a man standing by a white sedan. Ralph? The teen hippy was gone, replaced by a natty professor-type with a slight pot belly, wire-rimmed glasses and a bushy mustache. He'd traded in his tie-dyed shirt for a bowtie, his long blond hair pulled into a ponytail at the base of his neck.

He straightened as I approached. We stood a moment, staring at each other.

"Ralph," I said. "Thank you…for coming."

"Jared." He looked me up and down. "It's really you."

"Yes."

He didn't smile, nor did he frown. I couldn't gauge his reaction. "Get in," he said. "I've got a room booked at a motel nearby. We can talk there."

I got into the car. Ralph drove in silence to a motel with weathered green siding and a flickering neon sign that read *Ranc er's Inn.*

"Wait here."

I waited while he got a key from the office and then followed him to the room, taking in every small detail as if I were seeing the world for the first time: a white plastic chair coated in grime on the tiny porch. A stained ashtray on the plastic side table. Light blue door tinged with rust. The number 7 hanging by one nail.

A musty smell greeted us when we entered. Ralph switched on a light, revealing two double beds covered in stained, avocado green bedspreads.

"I didn't do this." I stayed in the doorway as Ralph threw his duffle on one of the beds and loosened his bowtie.

He turned and looked at me, blinked. "We'll get to that. I'm starving. Why don't you take a shower." He tossed me a small plastic bag from his duffle. "Some toiletries."

He used the room phone to call for a pizza. I took a shower while he made more calls, one to his lawyer, another to his father, Rafe. He didn't say much, mostly listened and said, "I know, I know, I will," once or twice.

The pizza arrived, and Ralph poured two glasses of water from the bathroom sink.

"Help yourself." He sat on the bed, picked up a piece and took a huge bite.

"No, thanks."

"You should eat something. You used to go for days without eating. I wondered how you survived sometimes."

I picked up a piece, took a bite, set it down. "How are your parents?"

"They're fine."

"Colette?"

"Died last year. Heart failure."

I dropped my gaze. "I'm sorry."

Colette. I remembered her as a baby. Now she was dead.

"Now that we're all caught up, tell me what happened. Your version."

I told him about my arrival at the ranch, about the weird ceremonies, about Brother X and Pris. I talked while he ate three pieces of pizza. He asked a few questions but made no comment nor any reaction.

When I was done, he closed the pizza box, wiped his mouth

and then looked me.

"Jared. Do you know what you are?"

I straightened, taken aback. "What do you mean?"

"This Brother X guy thought you were an angel. He wasn't all wrong about that."

"He was crazy."

"Crazy like a fox."

"What are you talking about?"

He sighed and got up, went to his duffle and rummaged around for a bit. He pulled out a tattered book. "In college, I studied ancient civilizations, with a minor in Biblical History—mainly because I wanted to know more about you. Colette gave me some hints, but even she didn't know the whole story."

"What did she tell you?"

"That you aren't really her son, which I had already figured out. That there was something odd about you, something that the family had striven for years to keep hidden. Something dangerous yet unspoken. I wanted to know what that was. After all, I saw you jump out of a fourth-story window and get up, virtually unhurt. That wasn't normal. In fact, it was downright unnatural. My father said you'd always been young, that you never seemed to age. And here we are—in ten years you've hardly aged at all. Also not natural, would you agree?"

I nodded.

"So I started doing my own research. I pored through all the family records, letters, anything I could get my hands on. I spent six months in France, tracking down our ancestors' birth and death records. And I found a birth certificate for Jean-Luc Laurent, September 2, 1859. That was you, wasn't it?"

"Yes," I murmured.

"At first, I thought, 'This makes no sense.' How could you be over a hundred years old? Then one day I read this curious scripture in the Bible, which I had somehow missed before. Listen." He opened the book to an earmarked page and read. "'When man began to multiply on the face of the land and daughters were born to them, the sons of God saw that the daughters of man were attractive. And they took as their wives any they chose. Then the LORD said, *My Spirit shall not abide in man forever, for he is flesh: his days shall be 120 years*. The Nephilim were on the earth in those days, and also afterward, when the sons of God came in to the daughters of man and they bore children to them. These were the mighty men who were of old, the men of renown.'"

He paused to look at me. "This is from Genesis, just before the Flood. You've heard of the Nephilim?"

I shook my head. I'd read the passage, but never paid attention to it.

"They are the offspring of angels and human women."

"That's not possible."

"Well, it is, actually. These angels—in other sources, they're called Watchers—manifested as humans—which angels are able to do—with all the human bodily functions necessary."

"Bodily functions?"

"Yes. Like eating and drinking and—" Ralph broke off and stared at me. "Jared, you know about men and women, don't you? About how…babies are born?"

I shook my head slowly. Ralph's eyes widened. Then he sighed. "You mean in all the years you've been alive, no one has ever explained that to you? Not even in the last ten years when you've been on your own?"

I shook my head. "I kept to myself, mostly. And before she died, my mother warned me to stay away from women, though I never knew why."

"Wow. That must be why you haven't changed yet."

"Changed? Ralph, I don't understand what you're saying."

"Okay, listen. These Nephilim were giants—the Bible calls them heroes, men of renown. It seems they were always male. They had superhuman abilities…incredible strength, things like that. And they must have lived a very long time, because it was after their appearance that God limited the age of men to one hundred twenty years and sent the Flood to destroy virtually all of mankind."

"What does that have to do—?"

"Hang on a minute. I'll explain." He flipped more pages to the back of the book. "There are several apocryphal books—not in the biblical canon—that relate to these giants. One of them is called the Book of Enoch. Listen to this." He read from the book. "'And they—that is, the women—became pregnant, and they bare great giants, whose height was three hundred ells: Who consumed all the acquisitions of men. And when men could no longer sustain them, the giants turned against them and devoured mankind. And they began to sin against birds, and beasts, and reptiles, and fish, and to devour one another's flesh, and drink the blood—'"

"Stop," I said. "I don't want to hear this."

"You have to hear this." He took off his glasses. "This is who you are."

Heat prickled my skin, seeping into muscle and bone. I could barely breathe.

"Your natural father was probably one too—how did he die?"

"Jumped off a building."

"Ah. That makes sense. The Nephilim are given to extreme behavior, psychosis—"

"Are you actually saying that I'm…one of those things?"

He took a breath and nodded. "I suspect still in the larvae stage. Meaning you haven't yet fully blossomed."

"But what you just read—I don't eat flesh. I don't drink blood."

"Not yet. But you will."

I dropped my head into my hands. As much as I wanted to deny this, it did explain a lot of things.

"Your healing power, your perpetual youth, the way music affects you—all marks of an angelic ancestry. I've got mountains of evidence."

"Please stop."

"I'll just summarize the salient points. The Nephilim might have started out as heroes, but they ended up as monsters, corrupting all flesh and wreaking havoc over the whole earth. The archangels complained to God, so God sent the Flood to destroy the earth and start over. The Watchers were cast into a deep pit in the earth—the Abyss. But somehow or other, the Nephilim reappeared after the Flood."

"How can that be? Everything was destroyed except for Noah's family."

"There are some theories. One is that the Nephilim genetic line continued through one of Noah's son's wives. There were eight people on the ark. In the Bible, seven is the number of completion, but eight is the number of resurrection. Rebirth. Regeneration. Could be a clue. The other theory is that the Watchers escaped from the Abyss and created more Nephilim after the Flood. Either way, when the Israelites entered the Promised Land two thousand years later, the giants were still around. They plagued Canaan right up until the conquest. Moses, Joshua and even David had to battle with them. You know the story of Goliath?"

"He was a Nephilim?"

"One of the descendants, known as Rephaim. There were other giant races as well—Anakin, Zamzummin, Emin, all originating from the Nephilim. David finally defeated the Rephaim tribes and drove them out of the land. But there was a remnant—there is always a remnant. It is believed they went north, into Europe and Scandinavia and established new kingdoms, new empires. Much of the Norse mythology is derived from their legends."

"Baldyr," I murmured.

"What did you say?"

"Colette believed I was Baldyr."

Ralph's eyes widened. "The Norse god?"

"It's why we left France. She thought the Nazis were going to try and find me. That Baldyr was like their messiah."

"Ah. That makes sense now. Curse our tight-lipped family. Secrets are the death of us." He paused, picking at his beard thoughtfully.

"But the Watchers are in prison…right? In the Abyss?"

"Yes. Though they still have influence, through demonic spirits."

*Shadow people.* I closed my eyes. "Do you know their names?"

"Not all of them. There were two hundred, initially. The leaders were Samyaza and Azazel—"

"Azazel?" I open my eyes.

"You know that name?"

"He… speaks to me," I whispered. "He calls me…his son."

Ralph was silent.

"That's why he tried to kill me," I murmured.

"Who?"

"My father. When he jumped off Notre Dame, I was on his back."

Ralph's eyebrows lifted in surprise. "But you survived. Interesting. Your blood is far stronger than his. Most of the males in our family tended to die young through violent means—perhaps that is a blessing for the world. But your natural father married a carrier nearly as pure as himself."

"A carrier?"

"Those of us who don't display the qualities of a true specimen still carry the genetic markers to varying degrees. Your parents were circus performers—they were good?"

"The best."

"A common characteristic of carriers—in addition to exceptional strength, pronounced artistic ability. Explains your musical talent. Thankfully, I was spared all that. Not an artistic bone in my body."

I told him about the old man who had spoken to my mother. He nodded and leaned back against the headboard. "We are one screwed-up family." He laughed to himself. "When I heard about what had gone on at that ranch, I was sure you were responsible. You see why? It's in your nature."

"But I didn't do it. I was a prisoner there."

"A prisoner? You could have escaped. I'm guessing that you are even stronger now than you were ten years ago."

"I should have," I admitted. "But I wanted to—stop him."

"You mean about the girl, Pris?"

"Yes."

"What you should have done was left the ranch and reported that to the Mounties."

"I told the detective. But he didn't believe me."

Ralph sighed. "My lawyer will be here tomorrow. We'll do what we can to find out the truth. This may be a long battle. I hope you're ready."

"I'm ready."

He yawned and stretched out on the bed. "I told my father you had called me. He advised me not to get involved. That you were—a lost cause."

"Why *did* you come?"

"I kept thinking about those times, remember? Going to the

circus. To the falls. The good times. You rescued me from a vicious dog once, remember that?"

"Yes."

"I just couldn't let you hang out to dry all alone."

"Thank you. For coming."

"You're still my big brother, eh?" He grinned. "My *younger* big brother, anyway."

# Chapter Seventeen

I'd been charged with drug trafficking and conspiracy to murder.

Brother X was released.

A mental exam proved him completely sane. The police believed his story of religious persecution. Believed I broke his jaw after he tried to stop the crucifixion reenactment. They believed that I was the one in control. All the witnesses backed him up.

That's what the lawyer told us when he came to our motel room, where we were hiding out from the press. His name was Dillon Straithan, and he'd gone to college with Ralph, though he was a year or two older. He didn't look much like a lawyer—he wore an open collar shirt and an earring in one ear. He was accompanied by a young woman with a mannish haircut and plump figure, whom he introduced as his private investigator, Emilia. She shook my hand with a kind smile. She wore a bulky sweater in a multitude of colors—I had a strong suspicion she knitted it herself.

She took notes as I recounted the past ten years, drifting from ranch to ranch, being paid in cash and moving on. It didn't help my defense. Cult leaders often started out as drifters. And I didn't remember the names of anyone I worked for. I had no alibi.

"I saw the interview tapes with Brother X," Dillon said. "Pretty convincing. He came across as a bumbling old man, totally under the control of his young protégé, the boy he'd rescued from the streets of Vancouver and raised as his own son."

"It's a lie," I said.

"The witnesses tell the same tale."

"What about Pris? Priscilla?"

"Her too."

My mouth dropped open. "She can't. I mean, she's lying."

"Trying to prove a hundred people are all lying is a pretty tough job, eh?" Dillon chuckled. "Look, Jared, if you told the truth, you might be able to cut a deal—"

"I am telling the truth."

He sighed. "Do you have anything that can help us defend you? Any useful information?"

"Well...Aaron told me that none of the adults were allowed to get married. That Brother X was the father of all the children at the ranch."

"We could try to get blood tests, confirm paternity," Emilia suggested.

"The court will refuse," said Dillon. "Not enough cause. Besides, it's not technically illegal, if all parties are consenting."

"What if they weren't?" says Ralph. "Jared, when you saw Pris come out of the house, you said she was bent over and crying?"

"Yes."

Ralph looked at Dillon, who nodded.

"What are you thinking?" I asked.

"That he didn't just beat that girl," said Dillon. "He raped her."

I stared.

"He doesn't know what that means," Ralph said. "Jared may look like an adult, but he's...not."

They then proceeded to explain it to me.

I should have been horrified. Instead, I was angry. Anger was the one thing I could feel utterly, completely. Anger that I had been so deceived. Anger at my own ignorance. That Brother X was planning to use me to serve his depraved desires. And I almost let him do it.

"If he was doing this routinely," Dillon said, "then clearly it was not consensual. And you said there was another little girl on the way to the house that night?" I nodded. "Do you know her name?"

"No."

"But none of the girls have even admitted to being beaten, let alone sexually assaulted," said Emilia.

"That's not uncommon in cults," said Dillon. "But we won't be able to prove it if we don't get one of them to come forward."

"What about the woman Jared mentioned in the police report," said Emilia. "Mimi?"

"She practically ran everything at the ranch," I said. "But the detective claimed he never heard of her."

"I'll start looking." Emilia seemed supremely confident. "If she's in the wind, I'll find her."

—

My appearance at the courthouse the following day was a media circus, probably the biggest news to come out of the Canadian Prairie in a hundred years. A huge cluster of Brother X's followers chanted *Justice for Brother X!* as I passed by, trailed by a caravan of camera crews.

"This is not just the legal system arrayed against you," Ralph said as we walked up the courthouse steps. "There are spiritual forces at work here."

"I know," I said. "I see them. Hear them. Including him."

"Him?"

"Azazel."

The prosecutor dropped the murder charges against me for lack of evidence and because several Mounties saw me tackle Aaron. I pled not guilty to the drug charges and was given house arrest until the trial, as I was not considered a flight risk, and Dillon argued successfully that I would be in danger in prison. It was victory, albeit a small one.

I saw Pris standing with the Bees as I left the courthouse. She was the only one not chanting. I stopped and called to her. "Pris! Tell them the truth!"

She stared at me a moment, then looked away.

—

"So far, no Mimi." Back in the motel, Emilia stood in front of the window, her stocky girth blocking the attempts of reporters to get a peek inside. "I'm thinking maybe she's the one who called in the tip to police."

"I thought she was his right hand," said Dillon.

"Maybe she saw the light."

"There could be another reason," I said.

"What's that?" Dillon asked.

"I don't know for sure, but I think Pris is… her daughter."

All three of them stared at me. Dillon said: "Her daughter?"

"They looked similar. And the way Mimi treated her… Maybe what Brother X did to Pris was the last straw."

Ralph sighed. "If she did call in that tip, she must be in hiding."

"Maybe we can draw her out," said Dillon. "We can make a public appeal. Call a press conference. Jared can ask her to come forward and testify. We could get the judge to offer her immunity and protection."

"Can you do that, Jared?" Ralph asked. "Go on television?"

I hesitated. My mother's voice rang in my ears: *Hide yourself.* But there seemed no other choice.

～

We held the press conference at the courthouse—reporters crammed the room, their cameras flashing nonstop. I sat behind a cluster of microphones and unfolded a piece of paper with my message. The shadow people closed in—they loved spectacles such as this.

I cleared my throat. My voice echoed in the multitude of mics. I forced myself to breathe evenly, to stay calm.

"Thank you for coming. I want everyone to know I am innocent. I was held prisoner by the man who goes by the name Brother X. He is a cult leader and a child abuser. Everything he has said about me is a lie." I looked up, directly into the cameras. "I ask the woman called Mimi to step forward, to tell the truth. She knows what really happened. Mimi, if you are listening to this, if you are watching, please. Tell the truth. You have the power to end this. To put Brother X away for the crimes he has committed. You will have full immunity and protection. And that goes for anyone from the ranch who comes forward to tell the truth." I folded up the paper. "Thank you."

The room erupted—Dillon took over, answering questions

and offering a special phone number for those willing to speak out. Afterward, Dillon said I did well, that I was appealing and sincere and people would believe my story.

But the shadow people were at work, drowning out the truth in a tidal wave of lies.

Brother X held his own press conference. We watched it on television at the motel. He continued his confused-old-man act, which was alarmingly believable. He spoke of my extraordinary strength and how I would beat him or anyone who refused to follow my orders. He had the broken jaw to prove it. Then he broke down and cried real tears as the camera zoomed in on his face.

"What now?" I said after Ralph turned off the television in disgust.

The lawyer shrugged. "We stick to our game plan. The truth will come out. It always does. Eventually."

"How long will it take?"

He didn't answer.

# Chapter Eighteen

Mimi did not call, even though my appeal played over and over on television throughout the week. Nor did Emilia have any luck finding her.

"I don't know what to tell you." She shook her head. Shrugged helplessly. "I've spent weeks looking, Jared. The trail is cold. I would declare her a missing person, except that no one from the ranch will even acknowledge she ever existed."

"I didn't make her up," I said stoically.

Both she and Dillon looked at me as if they weren't so sure. Maybe I was the crazy one. Maybe Mimi never actually existed at all—that she was just in my head.

The events of the past weeks became so muddled I began to believe I really was the monster Brother X made me out to be. That I had reimagined reality to make myself seem innocent. Isn't that what evil people do? And according to Ralph and all the members of my family, I was born evil.

We had moved into a small, rented bungalow on a quiet street outside Calgary to await the trial. I was fitted with an ankle monitor so I couldn't leave the house. Not that I wanted to, for the front lawn was constantly infested with news crews waiting to pounce.

I craved my guitar, which had not been returned to me. I had no way to drown out the shadow people, besides humming to myself, a tune I thought I made up that seemed to quiet the voices, keep them at a distance. Ralph heard me humming one night and remarked on it.

"I remember that tune," he said. "You used to hum it all the time when I was little."

"You...remember that?"

"Of course. I said you should write a song. Did you?"

I shook my head.

Emilia turned out to be a wonderful cook and spent most of her time trying to get me to eat. I had no appetite. Ralph attempted to distract me with chess matches, which he always won, while Dillon held late-night strategy sessions, drinking black coffee and eating Emilia's signature banana bread. It felt good, in a way, to be with people who actually seemed to care about proving my innocence. But I had no interest in the trial or in mounting a defense. What would it matter, if Mimi didn't even exist and Pris refused to speak?

One rainy night, when I was awake as usual, roaming around the house, I looked out the window to a see a lone figure in a yellow raincoat standing on the sidewalk. At first I thought it was some intrepid reporter determined to catch me if I stepped outside for a breath of air. Then she lifted her head, and I saw her face. I raised the sash and called out. "Pris!" She gasped and looked around, ready to flee. "Come in! You're soaked!"

She shook her head. "I just wanted to see... if you're all right."

"I'm fine. Are you?"

She shrugged. "I also wanted to tell you that... I'm sorry."

"Don't be sorry. Just testify. Tell the truth."

I couldn't tell if she was crying, or it was only the rain streaking her face. "I don't know what's true anymore."

"You know I didn't have anything to do with this. And you know that your own father abused you." I paused. "Was that...the first time?"

She nodded, a sob rising from her throat.

"Listen, Pris, what he did was wrong. It was evil."

The shadow people hissed at me.

"Brother X says all forms of love are a gift from Jehovah."

"This isn't love, Pris. It's an abomination in God's eyes."

"Jehovah—"

"Brother X's Jehovah isn't God. It's some made-up thing he uses to justify his evil actions. Everything he's told you is a lie."

"He says you are the liar. That you caused Abby to fall into the creek so you could save her, so you could come into the ranch and mess up everything. That Satan disguises himself…as an angel of light."

"You think I'm Satan?" She chewed her lower lip but didn't answer. "Pris, do you pray?"

"Yes. All the time."

"Okay then. Pray. Talk to God, the *real* God. Ask him what you should do. Don't listen to me, don't listen to Brother X. Listen to His voice."

"How will I know it's really Him?"

"You'll know."

"Jared. I… I…"

"What?"

"I… have to go." She ran off into the dark night.

～

On the first day of the trial, journalists, Bees, gawkers and legions of shadow people crowded into the courtroom. Neither Pris nor Mimi were among them. Perhaps Pris had prayed, and God had told her to keep silent. It was God, I decided, who would convict me. I was born guilty.

In addition to the physical evidence, the prosecution had dozens of witnesses telling the same well-rehearsed story: I had controlled Brother X, I was the one who masterminded the drug business, the rituals, even the crucifixion. They spoke in wondrous tones of my transformation into a real angel, complete with glowing skin and wings. Dillon tried to expose their lies during the cross-examination, but they never wavered.

In a way, I understood. They did see me actually glow, after all. Moreover, they had been conditioned to hate the outside world and distrust the government—they would never betray their own. Whatever they knew or didn't know about Brother X, they were united against the society they had abandoned—the society doomed to destruction in the coming nuclear war.

I sat silent and stoic through it all, too numb to register any of it. My lack of emotion probably convicted me in the mind of the jury. But it was like the witnesses were talking about someone else, not the person I thought I was but the creature I would become.

Brother X was the last to testify. The packed courtroom sizzled with palpable excitement as he shuffled to the witness box, slumped-shouldered like a man twice is age. His jaw was no longer bandaged, but he had let his beard grow long and scraggly, and his eyes shifted constantly, red-rimmed and deeply lined. He spoke not in his melodious tenor but in a fumbling, stuttering bass, detailing all the ways I had mesmerized him, bent him to my will. That it happened slowly, over the years, me putting thoughts into his head, words into his mouth. He had finally come to realize that I was not his beloved Jehovah, but actually the devil in disguise. He wept real tears as if overcome with sorrow for his dreadful mistake.

Dillon rose to cross-examine him. "Mr. Langston, we have testimony from several of the men that you were the only one allowed to have marital relations with any of the women at the ranch. Is that true?"

Brother X nodded. "Yes, it's true. Everyone who joined the community agreed to that. It was Jehovah's command. To keep the bloodline pure."

"So only your bloodline is pure?"

"According to what he told me—him!" He pointed to me. "If I'd only known what he really was!" He lowered his head.

"Did Jehovah also tell you to sexually abuse your own children?"

Langston's eyes grew wide. "I never did that!"

"And you've so thoroughly brainwashed them that they refuse to turn you in!"

"Objection! Badgering!" barked the prosecutor.

"No, no, I would never do such a thing to my own children! I loved them! I loved them!" Langston became so distraught that the judge insisted he be dismissed. Langston went back to sit in the gallery, consoled by his beloved Bees. The shadow people hooted with pleasure.

The prosecution rested. It was our turn.

Dillon stood and called Pris's name. I looked around, absurdly hopeful. No one in the courtroom moved. Dillon called her name again. After a few more minutes of silence, he called Mimi's name.

No sound but the shuffling and murmuring of spectators growing impatient. I dropped my eyes to my lap. It was over.

"I'm here." A small voice rose from the back of the courtroom. A slip of a girl in a yellow raincoat walked down the center aisle, past the glittering stares of her sisterhood and the hard blue gaze of her father. She didn't look left or right, just walked through the barrier and into the witness box. A bailiff came forward and made her swear to tell the truth. She ended with, "So help me, Jehov…God."

"What is your name?" Dillon asked.

"Pris. Priscilla."

"Could you speak up, please?"

She raised her chin. "Priscilla."

"Last name?"

"I…I don't have one."

"Where do you live?"

"Promise Ranch."

"Priscilla, can you tell the jury what happened to you on the night in question?"

"I was…woken up by Eli, one of the guardians…"

"Objection!" the prosecutor barked. "What does this child's testimony have to do with the defendant's actions in this trial?"

"Please, Your Honor," Dillon said. "Priscilla's testimony is vital to proving that Brother X was abusing minor children, his *own* children."

"Proceed," the judge said.

"Thank you, Judge," said Dillon. "Please continue, Priscilla."

"Eli told me that Brother X wanted to see me. I thought I was in trouble because I'd taken some marijuana from the storehouse and my friend Abby and I went to the woods to smoke it—we were supposed to be collecting herbs." Her voice grew stronger as she talked. "I got in the car and was driven up a mountain to a big house. I'd never been there before. It was this beautiful mansion. And Eli brought me inside where Brother X was waiting for me." She paused to clear her throat. Her voice began to shake. "He told me he knew what I'd done, and I had sinned. I had to pay for my sin. I was scared because I thought he was going to whip me. I'd heard other people got whipped when they disobeyed. I tried to apologize, I promised never to do it again. And then he told me to…take off my clothes and…lie down…" She started to cry. "He made me…do things. It hurt. I cried. I begged him to stop. But he said it was because he loved me and this was the only way Jehovah would forgive me…"

The courthouse was deadly silent as she wept. I closed my eyes, forcing down the rage that threatened to set my body ablaze.

"Do you want a few minutes to compose yourself?" Dillon asked gently.

She shook her head. "I'm…okay."

"Tell me…that moment at the creek, that was the first time you ever saw my client, Jared Laurent, right?"

"Yes."

"He'd never been to the ranch before."

She shook her head. "I'm sure I would have noticed him. He's hard…not to notice. Besides, Mimi didn't know him either."

"Mimi?"

"She was like…in charge of the ranch."

Dillon glanced at me—I let out a breath. Mimi did exist. I wasn't crazy.

Dillon asked: "Have you seen Mimi? Since that day of the raid?"

She shook her head. "No. I haven't."

"When was the last time you saw her?"

Pris paused to think. "Maybe at supper the night before everything happened? She was with Jared."

"So, you didn't see her the morning of the…crucifixion re-enactment?"

"I don't think so."

"Wasn't that unusual?"

"I guess so. She was usually with Brother X. But that day…everything was different."

"I see. No further questions. Thank you, Pris." Dillon sat down, glanced at me and smiled.

"Counselor?" the judge turned to the prosecutor.

"Just one question." The prosecutor stood up but remained at the table. "Priscilla, did you love Brother X?"

Pris's face seemed to crumple. Her eyes flicked to Brother X. "Yes."

"Do you think he would do anything to you that would be

wrong? To hurt you?"

"I never did—"

"So this story you told us about being abused by Brother X, aren't you really just covering up for the fact that it was you who stole the marijuana? That it was you who lured Abigail into the woods to smoke it? And it was you who caused your friend's near drowning?"

Pris burst into tears. "No, no, that's not it..."

"But you are guilty of those things, aren't you?"

"Yes, but..."

"And this young, handsome man here came along and bewitched you—and you wanted to help him out of his jam, didn't you?"

"No, that's not...I mean, I don't know..."

"No further questions." The prosecutor sat down. Pris sobbed softly as she was led from the witness box, mumbling words too garbled to understand.

I glanced at Ralph, who shrugged and pursed his lips as if to say, "Well, that could have gone better." I wrote a quick note and passed it to Dillon: *Someone needs to protect her.* Dillon read it, nodded, handed the note to Emilia, who followed Pris out of the courtroom.

The defense rested. The case went to the jury.

They took less than an hour to return with a verdict.

Guilty.

# Chapter Nineteen

I awaited sentencing at the jail. I felt calm inside, almost at peace, as if this was the proper outcome. God had spoken. Justice had spoken. I'd be better off in prison.

Dillon and Ralph came to visit me.

"We'll appeal," Dillon said. "Now that we know Mimi is…a real person…"

I shook my head. "She's dead."

"What?" Dillon's eyebrows lifted.

"He killed her. Or had her killed. Pris said she hasn't seen her since that day. Mimi would never have abandoned her own daughter. I think Brother X's white-shirts killed her and buried her body somewhere on the property. It's sixty thousand acres."

"Going to be hard to get a search warrant." Dillon shook his head. "But don't give up hope, Jared. We will fight this, even if it takes years."

⁓

I was sentenced to twenty years solitary confinement and sent to Edmonton Max. I don't remember much about the next five years. I slept sometimes, ate sometimes, paced the cell, looked out the window. Read books. Read the Bible cover to cover many times, along with the Book of Enoch, the Book of Giants, all the books that had anything to do with Nephilim. How long would it take for the change to occur, for an angel to turn into a demon? I wanted to be prepared.

Once a week I was allowed into the yard for exercise. I could glimpse the sky beyond the razor-wired walls, sometimes even the tips of a mountain on a clear day. I could have escaped, scaled the wall, outrun the guards. I would probably survive a gunshot, as long as it wasn't directly in my heart or brain. Every time I went into the yard I planned my escape, every muscle in my body twitching with the urge to do it. The shadow people constantly nagged me. *Doitdoitdoitdoit.*

I never did. My inaction was not based in fear. I simply had nowhere to go. Freedom was the only thing that frightened me.

Ralph visited every month. He told me he had gotten Pris into a halfway house in Calgary. She was taking classes at a junior college and hoping to get her degree in counseling.

"She's going to be okay, Jared, thanks to you."

I nodded, relieved. At least, something good had come out of all this.

"What's Brother X up to?" I asked.

Ralph sighed. "He's back at the ranch with his Bees. The drug business has been shut down, but he has no shortage of followers, thanks to his newfound fame."

I sighed in resignation. This was the new normal of the world. Lies trumped truth. But how many more girls would have to suffer because of my stupidity?

"But we have a plan," Ralph went on. "I hired Emilia. To infiltrate the ranch."

"How can she do that?"

"By pretending to be a man, of course. Brother X keeps a close eye on the women, but he could care less about the men. He needed laborers. He's building some sort of ark."

"It's too dangerous."

"Emilia can take care of herself, let me tell you."

I shook my head. "Really, Ralph, I appreciate all you're trying to do but—"

"This is not about you, Jared. This is about those girls. You understand that, don't you? It's not that I don't care about you. But you are going to live a very long time. You'll still be a young man when you get out of prison, even if you serve your whole term. But those girls…they need to be saved."

I smiled. "Yes. Thank you, Ralph. Thank you."

He was right. Twenty years was nothing to me. This endless living had become a kind of torture—what would I do with all the empty years ahead? If I could have ended it all, I would have.

Then one day my prison guard, Ray—the only guard who ever spoke to me directly—handed me a newspaper through the cell bars. "Thought you might be interested."

I looked at the headline: *Cult leader charged with torture, murder.* My heart nearly stopped.

*Cult leader Jeremiah Langston, aka Brother X, was arrested and charged with the murder of a woman and the torture of several of his followers. A young woman who had escaped from the compound told a story of horror and mayhem…*

I let the newspaper drop to my lap as bile rose up to burn my throat.

Ralph came to visit the next day. We met in the "family room," as the prison guards liked to call it, and sat across from each other at a metal table. He told me what I couldn't bear to read.

"Emilia was there a couple of weeks when she befriended Abby—the girl you rescued from the creek."

"Abby was still there?"

"Yes. Almost all of them went back to Brother X—they had nowhere else to go, they didn't know any other life. Abby finally confided in Emilia—whom she knew as Paul—that Brother X had started a new method of sanctifying his Bees, at least the female ones: branding."

"*Branding?*"

Ralph nodded grimly. "She even showed off the brand on her thigh—a big letter X. A mark of protection from Satan, he said. Apparently he had convinced the hive that you were going to escape prison and come back and kill them all if they did not submit. He used that excuse to come up with even more vile ways to abuse his followers. Unspeakable acts."

Ralph closed his eyes a moment, as if trying to un-remember the things he had heard. "It took some time, but Emilia finally convinced Abby to leave. I don't know how she did it. Emilia masterminded the whole escape plan too. They left during the night, took one of the plow horses and rode ten miles to the next ranch over. The rancher called the Mounties."

"And they listened to her?"

Ralph nodded. "Abby had more information than the branding and the abuse. She knew where the bodies were buried. Including Mimi's."

"So, Mimi is dead."

"Buried in the floor of the drug building, which had been sealed off after the first raid. I suspect there were others who'd tried to escape and didn't make it."

"Lord."

"I called Dillon right away—he's submitting a motion to dismiss based on this new evidence. Jeremiah Langston is going down for good."

It seemed too good to be true. I waited for some sort of reversal, Azazel and his minions twisting everything again to keep me in prison. But the motion to dismiss was granted almost immediately. A month later, I walked out of the prison a free man. Ralph waited for me outside the gate, a guitar case in his hand. Dillon and Emilia stood on either side of him.

Emilia waved happily.

I hugged her. "Thank you."

"Don't thank me," she said. "It was the best day of my life when that evil monster was taken away in chains."

I turned to Ralph. He held out the guitar.

"Couldn't find your original one," he said. "But I hope this one will do."

I smiled, took the case. "Thanks."

"Well, brother, ready to go home?"

Home...something I never thought I would know until that moment, looking into the eyes of this man, my brother. I let out a long breath.

"Yes."

# Epilogue

In the years that followed, the story of Promise Ranch became the Thing we didn't speak about, ever. Not that it was totally out of our minds. My dreams—when I slept—were filled with Brother X holding high his glowing brand as young women begged for mercy. We learned he had been given a life sentence without parole. He hung himself in prison. I felt cheated—he should have suffered as he'd made his followers suffer. He got off easy.

Ralph got an occasional letter from Pris. She graduated from junior college, got a degree in counseling and worked as a guidance counselor in a high school. She got married eventually and had a child, a little boy she named Jared.

Abby moved in with Pris for a while after leaving the ranch. They joined a church and spent years discovering the real Jehovah and trying to heal. Abby overcame a severe drug addiction, and although she never married, she found refuge in art, painting beautiful portraits of the girls she remembered from Promise Ranch.

Ralph and I moved into a small house in Hamilton. Emilia moved in with us—Ralph hired her ostensibly as a housekeeper. He was a confirmed bachelor, but Emilia had many talents besides cooking, and Ralph seemed to think they would come in handy, especially with me around. We'd both learned to be on the lookout trouble—the battle was never over.

Years passed in relative peace. The story of Promise Ranch faded from public memory. After a while it seemed as if it had happened to someone else, another lifetime, which it kind of was.

Ralph taught ancient civilizations at the small college nearby. In the summers, we traveled all over the world, visiting the ruins of those civilizations and collecting rare and unusual artifacts for Ralph's burgeoning library. He changed our name to Lorn, a way of erasing the past, starting fresh.

And then I decided I wanted to go to school again. Ralph was against the idea—he'd made it his life's work to protect me from the forces that sought to overtake my soul. But he was encouraged by the fact that my "condition" had not progressed, and in the meantime it might be helpful for me to form some human bonds besides him and Emilia. So he enrolled me in a private prep school.

But the shadow people still clung to me. Within a year I was expelled for attacking another student with a fork. I had watched the student bully a younger boy for weeks in the lunch room, right under the noses of the teachers, who seemed to find it amusing. It wasn't that I cared so much about the boy who was bullied...I was just angry that the bullies seemed to get away with it unscathed. When I tried to intervene, one of them took a swing at me. He missed, but I didn't.

That's when Ralph told me he'd been offered a job at the State College in Buffalo, New York. "Why don't we go to America? Time for a new adventure."

So the three of us moved to Buffalo. Nearby the state college was a private high school called the Buffalo Academy of Arts, for gifted artists and musicians. I begged Ralph to let me go there, to give me another chance. I would be able to study music, the one thing that kept me sane. I wanted to play guitar in a group again, remembering my glory days in the Saint James Jazz Band and my favorite teacher, Holiday. The only time I'd really been happy.

Despite his reservations, Ralph enrolled me. BAA was the perfect hiding place for me. I could be a mostly normal kid, play my music, fill my days. I even managed to not get into trouble.

Until one day.

The school required students to take classes in other disciplines, so I took a drawing class where I met Derrick Holder, a tall, gawky kid who always dressed in black and wore eyeliner to look intimidating. Derrick's art was brilliant but terrifying—Dark Ones clung to him like leeches. I felt drawn to him, almost against my own will. Once he invited me to his house to play video games. I declined, told him I had practice. I felt bad because Derrick was a lonely kid, like me, and he needed a friend. He was the biggest misfit in a school full of misfits. I should have reached out, tried to help him. But I kept my distance—I had enough demons of my own.

Derrick didn't return to the school after Christmas break, and I'd heard he'd been suspended for hacking into the school's computer system. I forgot about him, until one cold day in January, when he burst through the emergency exit doors of the school atrium, brandishing a rifle.

My first instinct was to jump, which I did. Straight up into the catwalks above the atrium, as Derrick sprayed the room with bullets. I watched the screaming, frantic students diving for cover as if I were watching a movie, something far removed from my own life.

But then I heard a song, a song that had been mapped in my mind for as long as I could remember, a song I had found myself humming in my head when I felt the Dark Ones shadowing my soul. The Song compelled me, pushed me into the heart of the story again, though I didn't even know where it was coming from. I jumped back down to the floor, over thirty feet, into the path of Derrick Holder and his gun.

That's when I saw a girl with red hair.

She was singing.

# About the Author

Gina Detwiler is the co-author of the bestselling *The Prince Warriors* series in addition to the *Forlorn* series. She also writes about angels, Nephilim, and other bizarre Bible stuff on her blog at gina-detwiler.com.

Follow on Instagram and Facebook @ginadetwilerauthor. She also loves to hear from readers, so write to her at 61 Ponderosa Court, Orchard Park, NY 14127.

# Dear Reader

If you enjoyed reading *Before*, I would appreciate it if you would help others enjoy this book, too. Here are some of the ways you can help spread the word:

Lend it. This book is lending enabled so please share it with a friend.

Recommend it. Help other readers find this book by recommending it to friends, readers' groups, book clubs, and discussion forums.

Share it. Let other readers know you've read the book by positing a note to your social media account and/or your Goodreads account.

Review it. Please tell others why you liked this book by reviewing it on your favorite ebook site.

Everything you do to help others learn about my book is greatly appreciated!

*Gina Detwiler*

# Acknowledgments

Without the suggestion of Dawn Carrington, Editor-in-Chief of Vinspire Publishing, this book would never have been written. The Lord works in wondrous ways. I was just settling into Lockdown Mode and struggling through the first draft of *Forbidden*, the fourth book in the *Forlorn* series, when Dawn suggested writing a prequel for Jared's backstory. I had sketched some ideas in my mind for the other books, but actually writing it all out became absolutely essential to the development of books 4 and 5 of the series. So thank you, Dawn. You are an absolute genius.

I also want to thank my beta readers, Mary Akers and Tammy Sherwood, for their invaluable help with the early drafts. Many thanks also to my editor for this project, Delia Latham, for her encouragement and guidance.

# Plan Your Next Escape!
## What's Your Reading Pleasure?

Whether it's captivating historical romance, intriguing mysteries, young adult romance, illustrated children's books, or uplifting love stories, Vinspire Publishing has the adventure for you!

For a complete listing of books available, visit our website at www.vinspirepublishing.com.

Like us on Facebook at
www.facebook.com/VinspirePublishing

Follow us on Twitter @vinspire2004

Follow us on Instagram @vinspirepublishing

and follow our blog for details of our upcoming releases, giveaways, author insights, and more!
www.vinspirepublishing.com/blog.

*We are your travel guide to your next adventure!*

Made in the USA
Middletown, DE
29 June 2021